Longman
Simplified English Series

THE CORAL
ISLAND

LONGMAN SIMPLIFIED ENGLISH SERIES

"I found myself lying on a bank of grass."

THE CORAL ISLAND

BY

R. M. BALLANTYNE

SIMPLIFIED AND ABRIDGED BY

J. M. WINTERBOTTOM, B.Sc., Ph.D.

AND

M. G. WINTERBOTTOM

ILLUSTRATED BY TECLA MARUS

LONGMAN

LONGMAN GROUP LIMITED
London

*Associated companies, branches and representatives
throughout the world*

© Longman Group Ltd 1931

First published 1931
Second edition (reset and re-illustrated) 1959
New impressions *1960; *1961; *1963 (twice);
*1964 (twice); *1965; *1966; *1970;
*1971; *1972; *1973 (twice);
*1974; *1975; *1976;
*1977; *1979

ISBN 0 582 52803 8

*Printed in Hong Kong by
The Hong Kong Printing Press (1977) Ltd*

Longman Simplified English Series

This book has been specially prepared to make enjoyable reading for people to whom English is a second or a foreign language. An English writer never thinks of avoiding unusual words, so that the learner, trying to read the book in its original form, has to turn frequently to the dictionary and so loses much of the pleasure that the book ought to give.

This series is planned for such readers. There are very few words used which are outside the learner's vocabulary[1]. These few extra words are needed for the story and are explained when they first appear. Long sentences and difficult sentence patterns have been simplified. The resulting language is good and useful English, and the simplified book keeps much of the charm and flavour of the original.

At a rather more difficult level there is *The Bridge Series*, which helps the reader to cross the gap between the limited vocabulary and structures of the *Simplified English Series* and full English.

It is the aim of these two series to enable thousands of readers to enjoy without great difficulty some of the best books written in the English language, and in doing so, to equip themselves in the pleasantest possible way, to understand and appreciate any work written in English.

---

[1] The 2,000 root words of the *General Service List of English Words* of the *Interim Report on Vocabulary Selection*.

Longman Simplified English Series

PRONUNCIATION GUIDE

THERE are very few proper names in this book. In pronouncing them the main thing is to put the accent or stress on the correct syllable. In the list, therefore, the accented syllable is marked thus: Golíath; this means that the accent is on the second syllable. *Avatea* and *Tararo* are marked as Englishmen would probably say them.

In a few cases rhyme-words are given in the second column. For example, *moral* after *Coral* means that the vowels have the same sound.

Avatéa	four syllables
Córal	moral
Díamond	try: three syllables
Golíath	go: by
Péterkin	
Pénguin	guin = gwin
Ralph	safe: *but often* Ralf (a *as in* hat)
Taráro	

PRONUNCIATION GUIDE

CONTENTS

CONTENTS

LIST OF ILLUSTRATIONS

CHAPTER I

THE STORM

WANDERING has always been, and still is, what I love to do, the joy of my heart, the very sunshine of my life. As a child, as a boy, and as a man, I have been a wanderer throughout the length and breadth of the wide, wide world.

My father had been captain of a ship, and when I was about twelve years of age I went to sea. For some years I was happy in visiting the seaports, and in coasting along the shores of England. But, while engaged in the coasting trade, I met with many seamen who had travelled to almost every quarter of the globe. Of all the places of which they told me, none pleased my thoughts so much as the Coral Islands of the Southern Seas. They told me of thousands of beautiful islands that had been formed by a very small creature called the coral animal; islands where summer reigned nearly all the year round; yet where, strange to say, men were wild, bloodthirsty savages. These accounts had so great an effect upon my mind that, when I reached the age of fifteen, I resolved to make a journey to the South Seas myself.

I had much difficulty in persuading my parents to let me go; but when I urged on my father that he would never have become a great captain if he had remained in the coasting trade, he saw the truth of what I said, and gave his consent. My father placed me under the charge of an old friend of his, a merchant captain, who was about to sail to the South Seas in his own ship, the *Arrow*.

It was a bright, beautiful, warm day when our ship spread

her sails to the wind and sailed for the regions of the south. The captain shouted; the men ran to obey; the noble ship bent over to the wind, and the shore gradually faded from my view, while I stood looking on with a kind of feeling that the whole scene was a delightful dream.

There were a number of boys in the ship, but two of them were my special favourites. Jack Martin was a tall, broad-shouldered youth of eighteen, with a handsome, pleasant, firm face. He had been to a good school, was clever and lion-like in his actions, but mild and quiet by nature. Jack was a general favourite, and had a special fondness for me. My other companion was Peterkin Gay. He was little, quick, funny, and about fourteen years old. But Peterkin's fun was almost always harmless, else he could not have been so much liked as he was.

" Hallo, young man! " cried Jack Martin, touching me on the shoulder the day I joined the ship. " Come below, and I'll show you your bed. You and I are to be companions, and I think we shall be good friends, for I like the look of you."

Jack was right. He and I and Peterkin afterwards became the best and truest friends that ever sailed together on the stormy waves.

I shall say little about the first part of our voyage. We had the usual amount of rough weather and calm; also we saw many strange fish rolling in the sea, and I was greatly delighted one day by seeing a number of flying fish come out of the water and fly through the air about a foot above the surface.

At last we came among the coral islands of the Pacific, and I shall never forget the delight with which I gazed—when we chanced to pass one—at the pure white shores, and the green palm trees, which looked bright and beautiful in the sunshine. And often did we three wish to be landed on one, thinking that we should certainly find perfect happiness there! Our wish was granted sooner than we expected.

A WRECK

One night, soon after we entered the tropics, an awful storm burst upon our ship. For five days the storm continued in all its force. Everything was swept off the decks except one small boat, and we all thought ourselves lost. The captain said that he had no idea where we were, as we had been blown far out of our course; and we were much afraid that we might get amongst the dangerous coral reefs, of which there are so many in the Pacific.

At daybreak on the sixth morning of the storm we saw land in front of us. It was an island circled by a reef of coral, on which the waves broke with great force. There was calm water within this reef, but we could only see one narrow opening into it. This opening we tried to reach, but before we reached it a great wave broke over the back of the ship, damaged it, and thus left us at the mercy of the waves.

" That's the end of us now! " said the captain to the men. " Get the boat ready; we shall be on the rocks in less than half an hour."

The men obeyed in silence, for they felt that there was little hope for so small a boat in such a sea.

" Come, boys," said Jack Martin, in a grave tone, to me and Peterkin, as we stood on the deck awaiting our fate. " Come, boys; we three shall stick together. You see, it is impossible that the little boat can reach the shore, crowded with men. It will be sure to turn over; so I mean rather to trust myself to a large oar. I see through the telescope that the ship will strike at the tail of the reef, where the waves break into the quiet water inside, so, if we manage to keep hold of the oar till it is driven over the waves, we may perhaps reach the shore. What say you, will you join me? "

We gladly agreed to follow Jack, although I knew by the sad tone of his voice that he had little hope; and indeed, when I looked at the white waves that broke on the reef and boiled against the rocks as if in anger, I felt that there was but a step between us and death.

The ship was now very near the rocks. The men were ready with the boat, and the captain beside them giving orders, when a great wave came towards us. We three ran forward to lay hold of our oar, and had only just reached it when the wave fell on the deck with a sound like thunder. At the same moment the ship struck, the mast broke off close to the deck and went over the side, carrying the boat and the men along with it. Jack seized an axe to cut our oar free, but, owing to the motion of the ship, he missed and struck the axe deep into the oar. Another wave, however, washed the oar free. We all seized hold of it, and the next instant we were in the wild sea. The last thing I saw was the boat turning over, and all the sailors in the angry waves. Then I lost my senses.

CHAPTER 2

THE CORAL ISLAND

ON recovering my senses, I found myself lying on a bank of grass, under the shelter of a rock, with Peterkin on his knees by my side, tenderly washing my face with water, and trying to stop the blood that flowed from a wound in my head. I slowly recovered, and heard the voice of Peterkin asking whether I felt better. Little by little the roar of the waves became louder and clearer. I thought about being left on a distant island far, far away from my native land, and slowly opened my eyes to meet those of my companion, Jack, who was looking anxiously into my face. I now raised myself on my arm, and putting my hand to my head, found that it had been cut rather severely, and that I had lost a good deal of blood.

" Come, come, Ralph," said Jack, pressing me gently back.
" Lie down, my boy; you are not right yet. Wet your lips with
this water. I got it from a spring close by. There now, don't
say a word," said he, seeing me about to speak. " I'll tell you
all about it, but you must not speak a word till you have rested
well."

" Oh! don't stop him from speaking, Jack," said Peterkin,
who, now that his fears for my safety were removed, busied
himself in building a shelter of broken branches to protect me
from the wind; which, however, was almost unnecessary, for
the rock beside which I had been laid completely broke the force
of the wind. " Let him speak, Jack; it's a comfort to hear that
he's alive, after lying there stiff and white for a whole hour. I
never saw such a fellow as you are, Ralph; you are always trying
to be funny. You've almost knocked out all my teeth, and nearly
killed me, and now you go trying to make us think that you are
dead. It is very wicked of you; indeed it is."

While Peterkin was talking like this, my mind became quite
clear again, and I began to understand what had happened.

" What do you mean by saying I've half-killed you, Peterkin?"

" What do I mean? Don't you speak English; or shall I say
it in French? Don't you remember——"

" I remember nothing," said I, " after we were thrown into
the sea."

" Be quiet, Peterkin," said Jack; " remember Ralph is not well.
I'll explain it to you. You remember that after the ship struck,
we three jumped over the side into the sea: well, I noticed that
the oar struck your head and gave you that cut, which made you
lose your senses, so that you seized Peterkin round the neck
without knowing what you were doing. In doing so you pushed
the telescope—which you held on to as if it had been your life—
against Peterkin's mouth——"

" Pushed it against his mouth! " cried Peterkin. " Say forced
it down his throat. Why, there's the mark of the edge on the
back of my throat at this moment! "

" Well, well, be that as it may," continued Jack, " you held on to him, Ralph, till I feared you really would kill him; but I saw that he had a good hold of the oar, so I tried my hardest to push you towards the shore, which by good fortune we reached without much trouble, for the water inside the reef is quite calm."

" But what has become of the ship, Jack! " said Peterkin. " I saw you climbing up the rocks there while I was watching Ralph. Did you say she had gone to pieces? "

" No, she has not gone to pieces, but she has gone to the bottom," replied Jack.

WHAT WE HOPE TO DO

There was a long silence after Jack ceased speaking, and I have no doubt that each was thinking of our strange case. For my part, I cannot say that my thoughts were very happy. I knew that we were on an island, for Jack had said so, but whether there were people on it or not, I did not know. If there should be people, I felt certain, from all I had heard of the South Sea Islanders, that we should be roasted alive and eaten. If it should turn out that there were no people on the island, I fancied that we should die of hunger. " Oh," thought I, " if the ship had only struck on the rocks, we might have done quite well, for we could have obtained food from her, and tools with which we could build a shelter; but now—alas! alas! we are lost! " These last words I spoke aloud.

" Lost, Ralph? " cried Jack, while a smile spread over his face. " Saved, you should have said."

" Do you know what *I* think? " said Peterkin. " I have made up my mind that it's fine—the best thing that ever happened to us, and the most splendid chance that ever lay before three young sailor-boys. We've got an island all to ourselves. We'll take possession in the name of the king; we'll go and enter the service of the black natives. Of course we'll rise to the top. You shall be king, Jack, Ralph, chief minister, and I shall be——"

" But suppose there are no natives? "

" Then we'll build a charming house, and plant a lovely garden round it, full of the finest tropical flowers, and we'll farm the land, plant, sow, reap, eat, sleep and be joyful."

" But to be serious," said Jack, with a grave face, checking Peterkin's way of making fun of everything, " we are really in rather an uncomfortable condition. If this is a desert island, we shall have to live very much like the wild beasts, for we have not a tool of any kind—not even a knife."

" Yes, we have *that*," said Peterkin, putting his hand in his pocket, from which he drew forth a small pocket-knife with only one blade, and that broken.

" Well, that's better than nothing. But come," said Jack, rising; " we are wasting our time in *talking* instead of *doing*. You seem well enough to walk now, Ralph. Let us see what we have got in our pockets, and then let us climb some hill and find out what sort of island we have been cast upon, for, whether good or bad, it seems likely to be our home for some time to come."

CHAPTER 3

COCONUTS AND OTHER THINGS

We now seated ourselves upon a rock, and began to examine our things. When we reached the shore, after leaving the ship, my companions had taken off part of their clothes and spread them out in the sun to dry; for although the wind was blowing fiercely, there was not a single cloud in the bright sky. They had also stripped off most of my wet clothes and spread them also on the rocks. Having put on our garments, we now searched all our pockets with all possible care, and laid their contents out on a flat stone before us. Now that we fully understood our condition, it was with great anxiety that we turned our pockets inside out in order that nothing might escape us. When all was collected together, we found that our worldly goods consisted of the following:

First, a small pocket-knife with a single blade, broken off about the middle and very worn, besides having two or three pieces out of its edge. (Peterkin said of this, with his usual fun, that it would do for a saw as well as a knife, which was a great advantage.) Second, an old brass pencil-case without any lead in it. Third, a piece of thin rope about six yards long. Fourth, a sailmaker's needle—a small one. Fifth, a ship's telescope, which I happened to have in my hand at the time the ship struck, and which I had held on to firmly all the time I was in the water. Indeed, it was with difficulty that Jack got it out of my hand when I was lying helpless on the shore. Sixth, a ring which Jack always wore on his little finger. In addition we had the clothes on our backs.

While we were examining these things and talking about them, Jack suddenly started and cried out:

" The oar! We have forgotten the oar! "

" What good will that do us? " said Peterkin. " There's wood enough on the island to make a thousand oars."

" Yes, Peterkin," replied Jack; " but there's a bit of iron at the end of it, and that may be of much use to us."

" Very true," said I, " let us go and fetch it "; and with that we all three rose and went quickly down to the beach. I still felt a little weak from loss of blood, so that my companions soon began to leave me behind; but Jack saw this, and, with his usual kindness, turned back to help me. The storm had suddenly died away, just as if it had blown hard till it dashed our ship upon the rocks, and had nothing more to do after that.

THE ISLAND

The island on which we stood was hilly, and covered almost everywhere with the most beautiful and richly coloured trees and bushes, of none of which I knew the names at that time, except, indeed, the coconut palms, which I knew at once from the many pictures that I had seen of them before I left home. A white, sandy beach lined this bright green shore, and upon it there fell the little waves of the sea. This last surprised me, for I remembered that at home the sea used to fall in huge waves on he shore long after a storm had died down. But on my looking out to sea the cause was at once seen.

About a mile distant from the shore I saw the great waves of the ocean rolling like a green wall, and falling with a long, loud roar upon a low coral reef, where they were dashed into white clouds of water. These clouds sometimes flew very high, and every here and there beautiful coloured bands were formed for a moment among the falling drops. We afterwards found that this coral reef stretched quite round the island, and broke the force of the waves before they reached the shore. Beyond this, the sea rose and tossed from the effects of the storm; but between the reef and the shore it was as calm and as smooth as a pond.

A LUCKY FIND

While we thus gazed we were surprised by a loud cry from Peterkin, and on looking towards the edge of the sea, we saw him dancing and jumping about, and ever and again pulling with all his might at something that lay upon the shore.

" What a funny fellow he is, to be sure! " said Jack, taking me by the arm and hurrying forward. " Come, let us go and see what it is."

" Here it is, boys; come along. Just what we want! " cried

Peterkin as we drew near, still pulling with all his power. " First class! "

I might say that my companion, Peterkin, often used very strange words, and that I did not always know the meaning of them.

On coming up we found that Peterkin was trying to pull the axe out of the oar, into which, it will be remembered, Jack drove it while trying to cut the oar free when the ship struck. The axe had remained fast in the oar, and even now all Peterkin's strength could not draw it out.

" Ah! that is good indeed! " cried Jack, at the same time plucking the axe out of the wood. " What good luck this is! It will be of more value to us than a hundred knives, and the edge is quite new and sharp."

" The handle certainly is strong! " cried Peterkin. " My arms are nearly pulled off."

We carried the oar up with us to the place where we had left the rest of our things, intending to burn the wood away from the iron at some other time.

" Now, boys," said Jack, after we had laid it on the stone which had on it all that we had, " let us go to the tail of the island, where the ship struck, which is only a quarter of a mile off, and see if anything else has been thrown on shore. I don't expect anything, but it is well to see. When we get back here it will be time to have our supper and prepare our beds."

" Agreed! " cried Peterkin and I together. We would have agreed to anything Jack had said, for he was older and much stronger and taller than either of us, and was a very clever fellow; I think he would have been chosen by people much older than himself for their leader, especially if they wished to be led on a bold attempt.

"Peterkin was trying to pull the axe out of the oar."

FOOD

Now, as we hurried along the white beach, which shone so brightly in the rays of the setting sun that it quite hurt our eyes, the idea suddenly came into Peterkin's head that we had nothing to eat except the wild fruits, many of which grew all round us.

" What shall we do, Jack? " said he, with a sad look. " Perhaps they may not be good to eat; they may kill us! "

" No fear of that," replied Jack; " I have observed that a few of them are like some of the fruits that grow wild on our own native hills. Besides, I saw one or two strange birds eating them just a few minutes ago, and what won't kill the birds won't kill us. But look up there, Peterkin," continued Jack, pointing to the head of a coconut palm. " There are nuts for us in all stages.'

" So there are! " cried Peterkin, who, not being very observant, had been thinking too much of other things to notice anything so high above his head as the fruit of a palm tree.

But whatever faults my young friend had, he could certainly move quickly. Indeed, the nuts had hardly been pointed out to him when he climbed up the tall trunk of the tree, and in a few minutes came down with three nuts, each as large as a man's head.

" You had better keep them till we come back," said Jack. " Let us finish our work before eating."

" So be it, captain; go ahead," cried Peterkin, putting the nuts down. "In fact, I don't want to eat just now, but I would give a good deal for a drink. Oh, that I could find some water! But I don't see the smallest sign of any about here. I say, Jack, how does it happen that you seem to know everything? You have told us the names of half a dozen trees already, and yet you say that you were never in the South Seas before."

" I don't know *everything*, Peterkin, as you'll find out before long," replied Jack, with a smile; " but I have been a great reader of books of travel all my life, and that has taught me a good many things that you, perhaps, do not know."

"Oh, Jack, that's all nonsense. If you begin to say you have learnt everything from books, I'll quite lose my opinion of you," cried Peterkin.

"Very well, Peterkin, we shall see," said Jack, stopping under the shade of a coconut tree. "You said you were thirsty just a minute ago; now jump up that tree and bring down a nut—not a ripe one, bring a green, unripe one."

Peterkin looked surprised, but seeing that Jack was in earnest, he obeyed.

"Now cut a hole in it, and put it to your mouth, old fellow," said Jack.

Peterkin did as he was told, and we both burst into laughter at the changes that instantly passed over his expressive face. When he had put the nut to his mouth, and thrown back his head in order to catch what came out of it, his eyes opened to twice their usual size with surprise, while his throat moved quickly in the act of swallowing. Then a smile and look of great delight came over his face. At length he stopped, and, drawing a long breath, cried:

"Wonderful! Perfectly wonderful! I say, Jack, you're a Briton—the best fellow I ever met in my life. Only taste that!" said he, turning to me and holding the nut to my mouth.

I immediately drank, and certainly I was much surprised at the delightful drink that flowed down my throat. It was extremely cool, and had a sweet, but sharp, taste. I handed the nut to Jack, who, after tasting it, said:

"Now, Peterkin, you unbeliever, I never saw or tasted a coconut in my life before, except those sold in shops at home; but I once read that the green nuts contained that stuff, and you see it is true!"

"And pray," asked Peterkin, "what sort of 'stuff' does the ripe nut contain?"

"A hollow centre," answered Jack, "with something like milk in it; but it does not satisfy thirst so well. It is, however, very good food, I believe."

" Meat and drink on the same tree," cried Peterkin; " washing in the sea, lodging on the ground—and all for nothing! My dear boys, we're set up for life; it must be the ancient Garden of Eden—hurrah!" And Peterkin tossed his straw hat in the air, and ran along the beach, shouting like a madman with delight.

We had now come to the point of rock on which the ship had struck, but did not find a single thing, although we searched carefully among the coral rocks, which at this place went out so far as nearly to join the reef round the island.

WE PREPARE FOR THE NIGHT

It was beginning to grow dark when we got back, so we put off our visit to the top of a hill till next day, and employed the light that yet remained to us in cutting down a quantity of branches and the broad leaves of a tree of which none of us knew the name. With these we erected a sort of house, in which we meant to pass the night. Having put leaves and dry grass all over the floor, we turned to thoughts of supper. But it now occurred to us, for the first time, that we had no way of making a fire.

" Now, there's a fix! What shall we do? " said Peterkin, while we both turned our eyes to Jack, to whom we always looked in our difficulties.

Jack did not seem to know what to do.

" There are stones enough, no doubt, on the beach," said he, " but they are of no use at all without a steel."

" Oh, I have it! " Peterkin cried, starting up. " The telescope —the big glass at the end will light a fire! "

" You forget that we have no sun," said I.

Peterkin was silent.

" Ah, boys, I've got it now! " cried Jack, rising and cutting a branch from a neighbouring bush, which he stripped of its leaves. " I remember seeing this done once at home. Hand me the bit of rope."

With the rope and branch Jack soon formed a bow. Then he cut a piece, about three inches long, off the end of a dead branch, which he pointed at the two ends. Round this he passed the rope of the bow, and placed one end against his body, which was protected from its point by a piece of wood; the other point he placed against a bit of dry wood, and then began to saw hard with the bow. In a few seconds the dry wood began to smoke; in less than a minute it caught fire, and in less than a quarter of an hour we were eating and drinking coconuts round a fire that would have roasted an entire sheep, while the smoke and flames flew up among the broad leaves of the palm trees over our heads, and cast a warm glow upon our leafy house.

CHAPTER 4

AT THE BOTTOM OF THE LAGOON

WHAT a joyful thing it is to awaken, on a fresh, glorious morning, and find the rising sun shining into your face! When I awoke on the morning after the ship struck, I found myself in this most delightful condition. Just at that moment I caught sight of a very small parrot. It was seated on a branch that overhung Peterkin's head, and I was quickly lost in admiration of its green and other brightly-coloured feathers. While I looked I observed that the bird turned its head slowly from side to side, and looked downwards, first with one eye then with the other. On glancing downwards I observed that Peterkin's mouth was wide open, and that this unusual bird was looking into it.

Peterkin used to say that I had no fun whatever in my nature, and that I never could understand a funny saying. In regard to the latter, perhaps he was right, yet I think that, when they were explained to me, I understood them as well as most people: but in regard to the former he must certainly have been wrong, for this bird seemed to me to be extremely funny; and I could not help thinking that, if it should happen to faint, or slip its foot, and fall off the branch into Peterkin's mouth, he would perhaps think it funny too! Suddenly the parrot bent down its head and uttered a loud cry in his face. This awoke him, and, with a cry of surprise, he sat up, while the foolish bird flew quickly away.

" Oh, you wicked bird! " cried Peterkin, making a face at the bird. Then he rubbed his eyes, and asked what time it was.

I smiled at this question, and answered that, as our watches were at the bottom of the sea, I could not tell, but it was a little past sunrise.

OUR MORNING SWIM

Peterkin now began to remember where we were. As he looked up into the bright sky, and drew in a breath of the fresh air, his eyes shone with delight, and he uttered a faint " Hurrah! " and rubbed his eyes again. Then he gazed slowly round, till observing the calm sea through an opening in the bushes, he jumped suddenly up, as if he had received a shock, uttered a loud shout, threw off his garments, and, rushing over the white sands, ran into the water.

The cry awoke Jack, who rose on his arm with a look of grave surprise; but this was followed by a quiet smile on seeing Peterkin in the water. Jack acted quickly only when he was moved, and on this occasion he jumped to his feet, threw off his clothes, shook back his hair, and, with a lionlike spring, dashed over the sands and into the sea, with such force as quite to cover Peterkin in a shower of water.

Jack was an extremely good swimmer and diver, so that after

he entered the water we saw no sign of him for nearly a minute; after which he suddenly came up, a good many yards out from the shore.

My spirits were so much raised by seeing all this that I, too, hastily threw off my garments and tried to jump to my feet as Jack had done; but my foot caught on a branch and I fell to the ground; then I slipped on a stone while running over the sands, and nearly fell again, much to the joy of Peterkin, who laughed loudly, and called me a " slow-coach," while Jack cried out, " Come along, Ralph, and I'll help you." However, when I got into the water I managed very well, for I was really a good swimmer and diver too. I could not, indeed, equal Jack, who was superior to any Englishman I ever saw, but I was very much better than Peterkin, who could only swim a little, and could not dive at all.

While Peterkin enjoyed himself near the shore and in running along the beach, Jack and I swam out into the deep water, and occasionally dived for stones. I shall never forget my surprise and delight on first seeing the bottom of the sea. As I have before said, the water within the reef was as calm as a pond; and, as there was no wind, it was quite clear from the surface to the bottom, so that we could see down easily even when the water was twenty or thirty yards deep.

IN THE LAGOON

When Jack and I dived in places where the water was not so deep, we expected to have found sand and stones, instead of which we found ourselves in what appeared really to be a wonderful garden. The whole of the bottom of the lagoon, as we called the calm water within the reef, was covered with coral of every shape, size, and colour. The most common kind was a sort of branching coral, and some portions were of a lovely pale pink colour, others pure white. Among this there grew large quantities of seaweed of the richest colours imaginable, and of the most graceful forms, while many fishes—blue, red, yellow and green—sported in and out amongst the flower-beds of this underwater-garden, and did not appear to be at all afraid of our approaching them.

On coming to the surface for breath, after our first dive, Jack and I rose close to each other.

" Did you ever in your life, Ralph, see anything so lovely? " said Jack, as he threw the water from his hair.

" Never," I replied. " It appears to me like fairy land. I can scarcely believe that we are not dreaming."

" Dreaming! " cried Jack. " Do you know, Ralph, I almost believe that we really are dreaming. But if so, I have made up my mind to make the most of it, and dream another dive; so here goes—down again, my boy."

We took the second dive together, and kept beside each other while under water, and I was greatly surprised to find that we could keep down much longer than I ever remember having done in our own seas at home. I believe that this was owing to the heat of the water, which was so warm that we afterwards found we could remain in it for two and three hours at a time without feeling any unpleasant effects such as we used to experience in the seas at home.

JACK SUPPLIES BREAKFAST

When Jack reached the bottom, he took hold of the branches of the coral and moved along on his hands and knees, looking under the seaweed and among the rocks. I observed him also pick up one or two large shell-fish and keep them in his hand, as if he meant to take them up with him, so I also gathered a few. Suddenly he put out his hand to seize a blue and yellow fish, and actually touched its tail, but did not catch it. At this he turned towards me and attempted to smile; but no sooner had he done so than he sprang like an arrow to the surface, where, on following him, I found that he had swallowed a good deal of water. In a few minutes he recovered, and we both turned to swim to the shore.

" I declare, Ralph," said he, " that I actually tried to laugh under water."

" So I saw," I replied; " and I saw, too, that you very nearly caught that fish by the tail. It would have done very well for breakfast, if you had."

" Breakfast enough here! " said he, holding up the shell-fish as we landed and ran up the beach. " Hullo, Peterkin! Here you are, boy. Open these while Ralph and I put on our clothes. They'll agree with the coconuts excellently, I have no doubt."

Peterkin, who was already dressed, took the shell-fish, and opened them with the edge of our axe, crying: " Now, that *is* fine! There's nothing I'm so fond of."

" Ah! that's lucky," said Jack. " I'll be able to keep you in good order now, Master Peterkin. You know you can't dive any better than a cat. So, sir, whenever you are not good, you shall have no shell-fish for breakfast."

" I'm very glad that our breakfast looks so good," said I, " for I feel as if I could eat a lot."

" Here, then, stop your mouth with that! " said Peterkin, holding a large shell-fish to my lips.

I opened my mouth and swallowed it in silence, and really it was very good.

We now set ourselves earnestly about our preparations for spending the day. We had no difficulty with the fire this morning, as the glass in our telescope was an admirable one; and while we roasted a few shell-fish and ate our coconuts, we held a long talk about our plans for the future.

CHAPTER 5

WE LOOK AT THE ISLAND

OUR first care, after breakfast, was to place the few things we possessed in a hole in a rock at the farther end of a small cave, which we discovered near our house. This cave we hoped might be useful to us afterwards as a store-house. Then we cut two large sticks off a very hard kind of tree which grew near at hand. One of these was given to Peterkin, the other to me, and Jack armed himself with the axe. We did this because we purposed to make a journey to the top of the mountains, in order to obtain a better view of our island. Of course we knew not what dangers we might meet by the way, so we thought it best to be prepared.

Having completed our arrangements and carefully put out our fire, we set out, and walked a short distance along the sea-beach till we came to the entrance of a valley, through which flowed a little stream. Here we turned our back on the sea and struck inland.

The view that burst upon our sight on entering the valley was truly splendid. On either side of us there was a gentle rise in the land, which thus formed two hills, about a mile on each side of the valley. These hills—which, as well as the low ground between them, were covered with trees and bushes—continued inland for about two miles, when they joined the foot of a small mountain. This mountain rose rather steeply from the head of the valley, and was also entirely covered, even to the top, with trees, except on one particular spot near the left shoulder, where there was a bare and rocky place of a broken and wild character. Beyond this mountain we could not see, and we therefore directed our course up the banks of the stream towards the foot of it, intending to climb to the top if that should be possible, as, indeed, we had no doubt it was.

JACK EXPLAINS MANY THINGS

Jack, being the wisest and boldest amongst us, took the lead, carrying the axe on his shoulder. Peterkin, with his great stick, came second, as he said he should like to be able to defend me if any danger should threaten. I brought up the rear, but having been more taken up with the wonderful and strange things I saw before we set out than with thoughts of possible danger, I had very foolishly left my stick behind me. Although, as I have said, the trees and bushes were very thick, they were not so close together as to stop our walking through them. Soon we arrived at the foot of the hill, and prepared to climb it. Here Jack made a discovery which caused us all very great joy. This was a tree of a beautiful appearance, which Jack declared to be the celebrated bread-fruit tree.

" Is it celebrated? " asked Peterkin simply.

" It is," replied Jack.

" That's odd, now," answered Peterkin; " I never heard of it before."

" Then it's not so celebrated as I thought it was," said Jack, quietly pushing Peterkin's hat over his eyes; " but listen, you little fool, and hear of it now."

Peterkin put on his hat again properly, and was soon listening with as much interest as myself, while Jack told us that this tree is one of the most valuable in the islands of the south; that it bears two, sometimes three, crops of fruit in the year; that the fruit is very like bread, and that it forms the principal food of many of the islanders.

" So," said Peterkin, " we seem to have every thing ready

prepared to our hands in this wonderful island—drink ready bottled in nuts, and bread growing on the trees! "

" Besides," continued Jack, " the bark of the young branches is made by the natives into cloth; and of the wood, which is hard and of a good colour, they build their houses. So you see, boys, that we have plenty of material to make us comfortable, if we are only clever enough to use it."

" But are you sure that that's it? " asked Peterkin.

" Quite sure," replied Jack, " for I was particularly interested in the account I once read of it, and I remember well what was said of it there. I am sorry, however, that I have forgotten what was said of many other trees which I am sure we have seen to-day, if we only knew them. So you see, Peterkin, I don't know everything yet."

" Never mind, Jack," said Peterkin, touching his tall companion on the shoulder. " Never mind, Jack; you know a good deal for your age. You're a clever boy, sir—a promising young man, and if you only go on as you have begun, sir, you will——"

The end of this speech was suddenly cut short by Jack pushing Peterkin into a mass of thick bushes, where, finding himself comfortable, he lay still, sunning himself, while Jack and I examined the bread-fruit tree.

THE BREAD-FRUIT TREE

We were much struck with the deep, rich green colour of its broad leaves, which were twelve or eighteen inches long, deeply toothed, and very smooth. The fruit with which it was loaded was nearly round, and appeared to be about six inches through the middle, with a rough skin. It was of different colours, from light green to brown and rich yellow. Jack said that the yellow was the ripe fruit. The bark of the tree was rough and light-coloured; the trunk was about two feet thick, and it appeared to be twenty feet high, there being no branches up to that height, after which it branched off into a beautiful head. We noticed that the fruit hung in groups of twos and threes on the branches, but as we were anxious to get to the top of the hill, we did not try to pluck any at that time.

Our hearts were now very much cheered by our good fortune, and it was with light, quick steps that we climbed up the steep sides of the hill. On reaching the top, a new and, if possible, a grander view met our gaze. We found that this was not the highest part of the island, but that another hill lay beyond, with a wide valley between it and the one on which we stood. This valley, like the first, was also full of rich trees. Among these we saw many bread-fruit trees with their yellow fruit; and also a great many coconut palms. When we had seen all that we could we went down the hill-side, and soon began to climb the second mountain. It was clothed with trees nearly all the way up, but the top was bare, and in some places broken.

FROM THE MOUNTAIN-TOP

We found this to be the highest point of the island, and from it we saw the country lying, as it were, like a map around us. It consisted of two mountains; the one we guessed at five hundred feet; the other, on which we stood, at one thousand. Between these lay a rich, beautiful valley, as already said. This valley crossed the island from one end to the other, being high in the middle and sloping on each side towards the sea. The large mountain sloped—on the side farthest from where the ship had struck—gently towards the sea; but although, when viewed at a glance, it had thus a regular sloping appearance, a more careful observation showed that it was broken up into many small valleys, mixed with little rocky spots and small but steep cliffs here and there, with streams falling over their edges and wandering down the slopes in little white rivers, sometimes shining among the broad leaves of the bread-fruit and coconut trees, or hidden altogether beneath the rich growth of bushes.

At the bottom of the mountain lay a narrow, bright green plain or meadow, which ended sharply at the shore. On the other side of the island, whence we had come, stood the smaller hill, from the foot of which started three valleys; one being that which we had come up, with a smaller valley on each side of it, and separated from it by the two low hills before mentioned. In these smaller valleys there were no streams, but they were clothed with the same rich growth of trees and bushes.

The island seemed to be about ten miles across, and as it was almost a circle in form, the distance round it must have been thirty miles—perhaps a little more, if we allow for the many bays. The entire island was surrounded by a beach of pure white sand. We now also observed that the coral reef completely circled the island, but it was not always the same distance from it; in some places it was a mile from the beach, in others a few hundred yards, but the usual distance was half a mile. The reef lay very low, and the clouds of water from the waves came quite over it in many places. These waves never ceased their war, for however calm the weather might be, there is always a gentle motion in the great Pacific, which, although scarcely noticeable out at sea, reaches the shore at last in a huge wave.

The water within the lagoon, as I have said, was perfectly still. There were three narrow openings in the reef: one opposite each end of the valley, which I have described as crossing the island, the other opposite our own valley, which we afterwards named the Valley of the Ship. At each of these openings the reef rose into two small green islands, covered with bushes and having one or two coconut palms on each. These islands were very strange, and appeared as if planted for the purpose of marking the way into the lagoon. Our captain was aiming at one of these openings the day the ship struck, and would have reached it, too, I doubt not, had not the ship been damaged. Within the lagoon were several pretty low islands, just opposite our camp; and immediately beyond these, out at sea, lay about a dozen other islands at distances from half a mile to ten miles—all of them, as far as we could see, smaller than ours, and apparently with nobody living on them. They seemed to be low coral islands, raised but little above the sea, yet covered with coconut trees.

All this we noted, and a great deal more, while we sat at the top of the mountain. Full of these discoveries, we came back to our house. On the way we came upon the footmarks of some fourfooted animal, but whether old or new none of us were able to say. This raised our hopes of obtaining some animal food on the island, so we reached home in good spirits, quite prepared for supper, and highly satisfied with our journey.

After much talk, in which Peterkin took the lead, we decided that there were no natives on the island, and went to bed.

CHAPTER 6

A SHARK

FOR several days after the journey which I have described above, we did not wander far from our house, but gave our time to forming plans for the future and making our present home comfortable.

There were various causes that led us to do so little. In the first place, although everything around us was so delightful, and we could without difficulty obtain all that we required for our comfort, we did not quite like the idea of settling down here for the rest of our lives, far away from our friends and our native land. Then there was a little uncertainty still as to there being natives on the island, and we had a kind of faint hope that a ship might come and take us off. But as day after day passed, and neither natives nor ship appeared, we gave up all hope of an early deliverance, and began to work hard at our home.

During this time, however, we had not been quite idle. We had several times tried, in different ways, to cook the coconut, but none of these improved it. Then we removed our goods, and made our home in the cave, but found the change so bad that we gladly returned to the house. Besides this, we swam very frequently, and talked a great deal; at least Jack and Peterkin did—I listened.

Among other useful things, Jack, who was always working at something, turned about three inches of the iron from the oar into an excellent knife. First he beat it quite flat with the axe. Then he made a rude handle and tied the iron to it with our piece of rope, and ground it to an edge on a piece of stone. When it was finished he used it to shape a better handle, to which he fixed it with a strip of his cotton handkerchief. The rope thus set free was used by Peterkin as a fishing line. He merely tied a piece of shell-fish to the end of it. This the fish were allowed to swallow, and then they were pulled quickly ashore. But as the line was very short and we had no boat, the fish we caught were extremely small.

OUR LOG BOAT

One day Peterkin came up from the beach, where he had been fishing, and said in a very cross tone: " I'll tell you what, Jack, I want you to swim out with me on your back, and let me fish in deep water! "

" Dear me, Peterkin," replied Jack, " I had no idea you were taking the thing so much to heart, else I would have got you out of that difficulty long ago. Let me see "—and Jack looked down at a piece of wood on which he had been working with a far-away look, which he always put on when trying to find a way out of a difficulty.

" What do you say to building a boat? " he asked, looking up quickly.

" Take far too long," was the reply; " can't wait. I want to begin at once! "

Again Jack considered. " I have it! " he cried. " We'll cut down a large tree, and put the trunk of it in the water, so that when you want to fish you've nothing to do but to swim out to it.'

This was agreed on, so we started off to a spot, not far distant, where we knew of a tree that would suit us, which grew near the water's edge. As soon as we reached it, Jack threw off his coat, and, with strong blows of the axe, cut at it for a quarter of an hour without ceasing. Then, while he sat down to rest, I continued the work. Then Peterkin made an attack on it, so that when Jack once more began to give it powerful blows, a few minutes' cutting brought it down with a terrible sound.

" Hurrah! " cried Jack. " Let us cut off its head."

So saying he began to cut through the trunk again, at about six yards from the thick end. This done, he cut three strong, short poles from the thicker branches, with which to roll the log down the beach into the sea; for, as it was nearly two feet thick at the large end, we could not move it without such helps. With the poles, however, we rolled it slowly into the sea.

Having thus been successful in getting our boat into the water, we next shaped the poles into rude oars, and then tried to get on. This was easy enough to do; but after seating ourselves on the log with one leg on either side, it was with the greatest difficulty that we kept it from rolling round and throwing us into the water. Not that we minded that much; but we preferred, if possible, to fish in dry clothes. To be sure, our trousers were necessarily wet, as our legs were in the water on each side of the log; but as they could be easily dried, we did not care. After half an hour's practice we were able to keep on the log fairly easily. Then Peterkin laid down his oar, and having put a whole shell-fish on his line, dropped it into deep water.

PETERKIN CATCHES A FISH

" Now then, Jack," said he, " be careful; keep away from that seaweed. There! that's it; gently now, gently. I see a fellow at least a foot long down there, coming to—— Ha! that's it. Oh, blow! he's off."

" Did he bite? " said Jack, sending the log on a little with his oar.

" Bite? Yes! He took it into his mouth, but the moment I began to pull he opened his mouth and let it out again."

" Let him swallow it next time," said Jack, laughing.

" There he is again! " cried Peterkin, his eyes shining. " Look out! Now then! No! Yes! No! Why, the fish *won't* swallow it!"

" Try to pull it up by the mouth, then! " cried Jack. " Do it gently."

A heavy sigh and a sad look showed that poor Peterkin had tried but that the fish had got away again.

" Never mind, my boy," said Jack; " we'll move on and offer it to some other fish."

So saying, Jack began to use his oar; but hardly had he moved from the spot, when a fish with a huge head and a little body rushed from under a rock and swallowed the shell-fish at once.

" Got him this time—that's a fact! " cried Peterkin, pulling in the line. " He's swallowed it right down to his tail, I declare. Oh, what a big one! "

As the fish came to the surface, we bent forward to see it, and the log turned round. Peterkin threw his arms round the fish's neck, and in another instant we were all in the water!

A shout of laughter burst from us as we rose to the surface like three drowned rats and seized hold of the log. We soon recovered our position, and sat more carefully, while Peterkin secured the fish, which had almost escaped during our struggles. It was hardly worth having, however; but, as Peterkin said, it was better than the little ones he had been catching for the last two or three days; so we laid it on the log before us, and having

"Peterkin dropped the line into the water."

put another shell-fish on the line, dropped it in again for another.

ATTACKED BY A SHARK

Now, while we were thus busy with our sport, our attention was drawn to a movement on the surface of the sea, just a few yards away from us. Peterkin shouted to us to row in that direction, as he thought it was a big fish and we might have a chance of catching it. But Jack, instead of doing so, said, in a deep, earnest tone of voice, which I never before heard him use:

" Pull up your line, Peterkin; seize your oar; quick—it's a shark! "

The fear with which we heard this may well be imagined, for it must be remembered that our legs were hanging down in the water, and we could not pull them up without the log turning over. Peterkin instantly pulled up the line, and seizing his oar, rowed his hardest, while we also did our best to make for the shore. But we were a good way off, and the log being, as I have before said, very heavy, moved but slowly through the water. We now saw the shark quite clearly, swimming round and round us. From its quick and unsteady movements, Jack knew it was making up its mind to attack us, so he urged us to row for our lives, while he himself set us the example. Suddenly he shouted, " Look out! There he comes! " and in a second we saw the great fish dive close under us, and turn half over on his side. But we all beat the water with our oars, which frightened it away for that time, but we saw it immediately after circling round us as before.

" Throw the fish to him! " cried Jack, in a quick, low voice. " We'll reach the shore in time yet, if we can keep him off for a few minutes."

Peterkin stopped one instant to obey the command, and then rowed again with all his might. No sooner had the fish fallen on the water than we observed the shark to disappear. In another moment his nose rose above the water; his wide mouth, armed with a fearful double row of teeth, appeared. The dead fish was swallowed and the shark disappeared again. But Jack was wrong in thinking that it would be satisfied. In a very few minutes it returned to us, and its quick movements led us to fear that it would attack us at once.

" Stop rowing! " cried Jack suddenly. " I see it coming up behind us. Now obey my orders *quickly*. Our lives may depend on it. Ralph, Peterkin, do your best to keep the log from turning over. Don't look out for the shark. Don't look behind you. Do nothing but keep the log from moving."

Peterkin and I instantly did as we were ordered, being only too glad to do anything that gave us a chance or a hope of escape, for we had great faith in Jack's courage and wisdom. For a few seconds, that seemed long minutes to my mind, we sat thus silently; but I could not help looking back, although I had been told not to. On doing so, I saw Jack sitting perfectly still, with his oar raised, his mouth shut closely, and his eyebrows bent over his eyes, which looked out fiercely beneath them down into the water. I also saw the shark, quite close under the log, in the act of rushing towards Jack's foot. I could hardly keep back a cry on seeing this. In another moment the shark rose. Jack drew his leg suddenly from the water and threw it over the log. The great head rubbed against the log as it passed, and we saw its huge mouth, into which Jack instantly pushed the oar, and drove it down its throat. So forceful was this act that Jack rose to his feet in doing it; the log was thus rolled completely over, and we were once more thrown into the water. We all rose in a moment.

" Now then, swim out for the shore! " cried Jack. " Here, Peterkin, catch hold of my collar, and swim as hard as you can."

Peterkin did as he was told, and Jack swam out with such force that he cut through the water like a boat; while I, having only myself to carry, succeeded in keeping up with him. As we had by this time drawn quite near to the shore, in a few minutes more we were in water not deep enough for the shark to swim in; and, finally, we landed in safety, though very tired and not a little frightened by this terrible affair.

CHAPTER 7

A GARDEN, SOME NUTS AND OTHER THINGS

OUR fight with the shark was the first great danger that we had met since landing on this island, and we were very much moved by it, especially when we considered that we had so often, without knowing it, run into the same danger before while swimming. We were now forced to take to fishing again in the water near the shore, until we should succeed in building a boat.

What troubled us most, however, was that we could no longer go for our morning swims. We did, indeed, continue to wash ourselves by the side of the sea, but Jack and I found that one of our greatest joys was gone when we could no longer dive down among the beautiful coral groves at the bottom of the lagoon. We had come to be so fond of this, and to take such an interest in watching the shapes of coral and the play of the many beautiful fish amongst the forests of red and green seaweeds, that we knew the appearance of the fish and the places where they were to be found.

We had also become very good divers. At times, when Jack happened to feel full of fun, he would seat himself at the bottom of the sea on one of the big pieces of coral, and then make faces at me, in order, if possible, to make me laugh under water. At first, when I was not expecting it, he nearly succeeded, and I shot to the surface in order to laugh; but afterwards I knew what he was trying to do, and being naturally of a grave nature, I had no difficulty in stopping myself.

I often used to wonder how poor Peterkin would have liked to be with us; and at times he expressed much sorrow at not being able to join us. I used to do my best to comfort him, poor fellow, by telling him of all the wonders that we saw; but this, instead of satisfying, seemed only to make him more anxious to come with us, so one day he agreed to try to go down with us. But although a brave boy in every other way, Peterkin was very afraid of the water, and it was with difficulty we got him to consent to be taken down, for he could never have managed to push himself down to the bottom without help. But we had only pulled him down a yard or so into the deep clear water when he began to struggle and kick, so we were forced to let him go, when he rose out of the water, gave a frightful roar, and struck out for the shore with the greatest possible haste.

Now all this pleasure we were to do without, and when we thought about it, Jack and I felt very sad. I could see, also, that Peterkin felt sorry for us, for when we talked about this matter he did not make fun about it.

THE WATER GARDEN

As, however, a man's difficulties usually set him upon trying to find a way to get out of them, so this, our difficulty, made us think of searching for a place among the rocks where the water should be deep enough for diving, yet so circled by rocks as to prevent sharks from getting at us. And such a place we afterwards found. It was not more than ten minutes' walk from our house, and was in the form of a small deep bay, the entrance to which, besides being narrow, was not deep enough for a fish so large as a shark to get in; at least, not unless he should be a very thin one.

Inside of this bay, which we called our Water Garden, the coral was much more wonderful, and the seaweed plants far more lovely and brightly coloured than in the lagoon itself. And the water was so clear and still that, although very deep, you could see the smallest object at the bottom. Besides this, there was a rock which overhung the water at its deepest part, from which we could dive pleasantly, and on which Peterkin could sit and see not only all the wonders I had described to him, but also see Jack and me creeping among the seaweeds at the bottom, like—as he expressed it—" two great white sea animals."

During these dives of ours to the bottom of the sea, we began to find out something of the manners and customs of the animals and to make discoveries of wonderful things, the like of which we never before thought of. Among other things, we were deeply interested in the work of the little coral animal which, I was informed by Jack, is supposed to have entirely made many of the islands in the Pacific Ocean. And certainly, when we considered the great reef which these animals had formed round the island on which we were cast, and observed the ceaseless way in which they built their coral houses, it did seem as if this might be true.

I also became much interested in the manners and appearance of other water creatures, and was not content with watching those I saw during my dives in the Water Garden. I made a hole in the coral rock close to it; this I filled with salt water, and put into it different shell-fish and other animals, in order to watch more closely how they passed their time. The big glass from our telescope also now became a great treasure to me, as by looking at the animals through it, they appeared larger, and so I could see more clearly the forms and actions of these strange creatures of the sea.

WE PLAN TO WALK ROUND THE ISLAND

Having now got ourselves into a very comfortable position, we began to talk of the plan which we had long thought of carrying out—namely, to travel entirely round the island; in order, first, to find out whether it contained any other things which might be useful to us; and, second, to see whether there might be any better place for us to live than that on which our house now stood. Not that there was anything about it which we did not like—in fact, we looked upon our house as a home— but if a better place did exist, there was no reason why we should not make use of it. At any rate, it would be well to know of it.

We had much earnest talk over this matter. But Jack said that, before starting on such a journey, we should supply ourselves with good arms, for as we intended not only to go round all the shore, but to go up most of the valleys, before we came home, we should be likely to meet with, he should not say *dangers*, but at least with everything there was on the island—whatever that might be.

" Besides," said Jack, " it won't be a good thing for us to live on coconuts and shell-fish always. No doubt they are very excellent in their way, but I think a little animal food now and then would be pleasant as well as good for us; and as there are many small birds among the trees, some of which are probably very good meat, I think it would be a fine plan to make bows and arrows, with which we could easily knock them over."

" First rate! " cried Peterkin. " You will make the bows, Jack, and I will make the arrows. The fact is, I am quite tired of throwing stones at the birds. I began the very day we landed, I think, and have kept on up to the present time, but I've never hit anything yet."

" You forget," said I, " you hit me one day on the leg."

" Ah, true," replied Peterkin, " and a great row you made about it. But you were at least four yards away from the parrot I was trying to hit; so you see what a bad shot I am."

" But, Jack," said I, " you cannot make three bows and arrows before to-morrow, and would it not be a pity to waste time, now that we have made up our minds to go on this journey? Suppose that you make one bow and arrow for yourself, and we can take our sticks? "

" That's true, Ralph. It is quite late, and I doubt if I can make even one bow before dark. To be sure, I might work by firelight, after the sun goes down."

We had, up to this time, been used to going to bed with the sun, as we had no real reason to work at nights, and, indeed, our work during the day was usually hard enough—what with fishing and improving our house, and diving in the Water Garden, and wandering in the woods—so that, when night came, we were usually very glad to retire to our beds. But now that we wanted to work at night, we felt a wish for a light.

" Won't a good fire give you light enough? " asked Peterkin.

" Yes," replied Jack, " quite enough; but then it will give us a great deal more than enough heat."

" True," said Peterkin; " I forgot that. It will cook us."

" Well," said Jack, " I've been thinking over this subject before. There is a certain nut growing in these islands which the natives use to give them a light, and I know all about it and how to prepare it for burning."

" Then why don't you do it? " said Peterkin. " Why have you kept us in the dark so long, you wicked fellow? "

PREPARATIONS

" Because," said Jack, " I have not seen the tree yet, and I'm not sure that I should know either the tree or the nuts if I did see them. You see, I forget what they were said to look like. I believe the nut is quite small; and I think that the leaves are white, but I am not sure."

" Eh! Ha! Hum! " cried Peterkin. " I saw a tree like that this very day! "

" Did you? " cried Jack. " Is it far from here? "

" No, not half a mile."

" Then lead me to it," said Jack, seizing his axe.

In a few minutes we were all three pushing through the bushes of the forest, led by Peterkin.

We quickly came to the tree Peterkin had told us about, which, after Jack had closely examined it, we concluded must be the right one. Its leaves were of a beautiful silvery white, very different from the dark green leaves of the trees round it. We immediately filled our pockets with the nuts, after which Jack said:

" Now, Peterkin, climb that coconut tree and cut me one of the long branches."

This was soon done, but it cost some trouble, for the trunk was very high, and as Peterkin usually pulled nuts from the younger trees, he did not often climb the high ones.

Jack now took one of the little leaves, and, cutting out the hard, stick-like middle, hurried back with it to our camp. Having made a small fire, he cooked the nuts slightly, and then took off the outsides. After this he wished to make a hole in them, which, not having anything better at the time, he did with the point of our pencil case. Then he put the middle part of the coconut leaf through the hole in each one, and on putting a light to the nut at the top, we found to our joy that it burned with a clear, beautiful flame. When he saw it, Peterkin jumped up and danced round the fire for at least five minutes.

" Now, boys," said Jack, putting out the light, " the sun will set in an hour, so we have no time to lose. I shall go and cut a young tree to make my bow out of, and you had better each of you go and select good strong sticks, and we'll set to work at them after dark."

So saying, he put his axe on his shoulder and went off, followed by Peterkin, while I took up a piece of coconut cloth and began to examine it. I was still occupied with this, and was sitting in the same position, when my companions came back.

" I told you so! " cried Peterkin, with a loud laugh. " Oh, Ralph, you're hopeless. See, there's a stick for you. I was sure, when we left you looking at that bit of stuff, that we would find you still looking at it when we came back, so I just cut a stick for you as well as for myself."

"Thank you, Peterkin," said I. "It was kind of you to do that, instead of being cross with me for being a lazy fellow, as I deserve."

" Oh, as to that," answered Peterkin, " I'll be cross with you yet, if you wish it; only it would be of no use if I did, for you'd still go your own way."

As it was now getting dark we lighted our light, and placing it in a holder, made of two crossing branches, inside our hut, we seated ourselves on our beds and began to work.

" I intend to keep the bow for my own use," said Jack, cutting with his axe at the piece of wood he had brought. " I used to be quite a good shot once. But what's that you're doing? " he added, looking at Peterkin, who had drawn the end of a long pole into the hut, and was trying to fit a small piece of iron to the end of it."

" You see, Jack," answered Peterkin, " I think I should like to have a spear."

" Well, if length is power," said Jack, " no one will be able to beat you."

The pole which Peterkin cut was fully twelve feet long, being a very strong but light young tree, which merely required thinning at one end to be a very good spear.

" That's a very good idea," said I.

" Which—this? " asked Peterkin, pointing to the spear.

" Yes," I replied.

" Hum! " said he. " You'd find it a very strong and real idea if you had it pushed through your body, old boy! "

" I mean the idea of making it is a good one," said I, laughing. " And, now I think of it, I'll change my plan too. I don't think much of the stick, so I'll make a sling out of this piece of cloth. I used to be very fond of slinging—ever since I read of David killing Goliath, the Philistine—and I was once thought to be very good at it."

A VERY STRANGE NOISE

So I set to work to make a sling. For a long time we all worked very busily without speaking. While we were thus engaged we were surprised to hear a distant but most strange and frightful cry. It seemed to come from the sea, but was so far away that we could not clearly tell its true direction. Rushing out of our house, we hurried down to the beach and stayed to listen. Again it came, quite loud on the night air. The moon had risen, and we could see the islands in and beyond the lagoon quite plainly, but there was no object that we could see to account for such a cry. A strong wind was blowing from the point whence the sound came, but this died away while we were gazing out to sea.

" What can it be? " said Peterkin, in a low voice, while we all crept close to each other.

" Do you know," said Jack, " I have heard that sound twice before, but never so loud as to-night. Indeed, it was so faint that I thought I must have merely fancied it, so, as I did not wish to alarm you, I said nothing about it."

We listened for a long time for the sound again, but as it did not come, we went back to the house and continued our work.

" Very strange," said Peterkin, quite gravely. " Do you believe in ghosts, Ralph? "

" No," I answered, " I do not. But I must say that strange sounds for which I cannot account, such as we have just heard, make me feel a little uneasy."

" What do you say to it, Jack? "

" I neither believe in ghosts nor feel uneasy," he replied. " I never saw a ghost myself, and I never met with anyone who had; and I have generally found that strange things have almost always been accounted for, and found to be quite simple on close examination. I certainly can't imagine what that sound is; but I am quite sure I shall find out before long, and if it is a ghost I'll —I'll——"

" Eat it! " cried Peterkin.

" Yes, I'll eat it! Now, then, my bow and two arrows are finished, so if you're ready we'd better go to bed."

By this time Peterkin had thinned down his spear, and tied an iron point very cleverly to the end of it; I had formed a sling, the lines of which were made of thin strips of coconut cloth; and Jack had made a bow, nearly five feet long, with two arrows, feathered with two or three large feathers which some bird had dropped. Jack said that if arrows were well feathered they did not require iron points, but would fly quite well if merely sharpened at the point, which I did not know before.

WE PRACTISE WITH OUR WEAPONS

Although thus prepared for a start on the next day, we thought it wise to have some practice in the use of our arms before starting, and on this we spent the whole of the next day. And it was well we did so, for we found that our arms were not at all perfect, and that we were far from perfect in the use of them. First, Jack found that the bow was much too strong, and he had to thin it. Also the spear was much too heavy, and so had to be made thinner, although Peterkin would on no account shorten it. My sling worked very well, but I was so much out of practice that my first stone knocked off Peterkin's hat, and narrowly missed making a second Goliath of him. However, after having spent the whole day in practice, we began to find some of our former cleverness returning—at least Jack and I did. As for Peterkin, being naturally good with his hands, he soon used his spear well, and was able to run as hard as he could at a coconut, and hit it in the middle once out of every five times.

But I think that we owed much of our rapid success to Jack, who said that, since we had made him captain, we should obey him, and he kept us at work from morning till night on the same thing. Peterkin wished very much to run about and stick his spear into everything he passed; but Jack put up a coconut, and would not let him leave off running at that for a moment, except when he wanted to rest. We laughed at Jack for this, but we both felt that it did us much good.

That night we examined and repaired our arms before we lay down to rest, although we were very tired, in order that we might be ready to start out on our journey at daylight on the following morning.

CHAPTER 8

STRANGE CLOUDS

HARDLY had the sun shot its first ray across the bosom of the broad Pacific, when Jack jumped to his feet, and, shouting in Peterkin's ear to wake him, ran down the beach to take his usual swim in the sea. We did not, as we usually did, go that morning to our Water Garden, but, in order to save time, washed ourselves in the lagoon just opposite the house. Our breakfast was eaten without loss of time, and in less than an hour afterwards all our preparations for the journey were completed.

In addition to his usual dress, Jack tied a belt of coconut cloth round his waist; into this he put the axe. I was also advised to put on a belt and carry a short stick in it; for, as I truly said, the sling would be of little use if we should chance to come very close to any wild animal. As for Peterkin, although he carried such a long, and I must add, frightful-looking spear over his shoulder, we could not make him leave his stick behind, " For," said he, " a spear, when close to an enemy, is not worth a button." I must say that it seemed to me that the stick was, to use his own language, not worth a button either; for the head was very rough, something like the stick which I remember to have seen in picture books of Jack the Giant-Killer, besides being so heavy that he required to hold it with both hands in order to use it at all. However, he took it with him, and in this manner we set out upon our travels.

We did not consider it necessary to carry any food with us, as we knew that wherever we went we should be certain to fall in with coconut trees; having these, we were well supplied, as Peterkin said, with meat and drink and cloth! I was careful, however, to put the glass from the telescope into my pocket, in case we should want a fire.

Half a mile's walk took us round a bend in the land which shut out our house from view, and for some time we advanced at a quick pace without speaking, though our eyes were not idle, but noted everything in the woods, on the shore, or in the sea that was interesting. After passing the hill that formed one side of our valley—the Valley of the Ship—we saw another small valley lying before us in all the loveliness of tropical plant life. We had, indeed, seen it before from the mountain-top, but we had no idea that it would turn out to be so much more lovely when we were close to it. We were about to begin to examine this valley, when Peterkin stopped us and directed our attention to a very strange appearance in front of us along the shore.

A PUZZLING SIGHT

" What's that, think you? " said he, levelling his spear as if he expected an immediate attack from the object in question, though it was quite half a mile distant.

As he spoke, there appeared a white cloud above the rocks as if of steam. It rose upwards to a height of several feet, and then disappeared. If this had been near the sea, we should not have been so greatly surprised, as it might in that case have been the waves, for at this part of the coast the coral reef approached so near to the island that in some parts it almost joined it. There was therefore no lagoon between, and the heavy waves of the ocean beat almost up to the rocks. But this white cloud appeared about fifty yards inland. The rocks at this place were rough, and they stretched across the sandy beach into the sea. Hardly had we ceased expressing our surprise at this sight, when another cloud flew upwards for a few seconds, not far from the spot where the first had been seen, and disappeared; and so, from time to time, these strange sights continued.

We were now quite sure that the clouds were watery, but what caused them we could not guess, so we determined to go and see. In a few minutes we gained the spot, which was very rough, and quite wet with the falling of the water. We had much difficulty in passing over with dry feet. The ground also was full of holes here and there. Now, while we stood anxiously waiting for the appearance of these clouds, we heard a low sound near us, which quickly increased to a loud noise, and a moment afterwards a thick cloud of water burst upwards from a hole in the rock and shot into the air with much force, and so close to where Jack and I were standing, that it nearly touched us. We sprang to one side, but not before the water came down and wetted us both to the skin.

Peterkin, who was standing farther off, escaped with a few drops, and burst into a fit of laughter on seeing our state.

" Mind your eye! " he shouted eagerly. "There goes another!"

The words were hardly out his mouth when there came up a cloud from another hole, which served us exactly in the same manner as before.

Peterkin shouted with laughter; but his joy was quickly ended by the noise occurring close to where he stood.

"Where will it come up this time, I wonder? " he said, looking anxiously about, and preparing to run.

Suddenly there came a loud noise; a fierce cloud of water burst between Peterkin's legs, blew him off his feet, surrounded him with water, and threw him to the ground. He fell with so much force that we feared he must have broken some of his bones, and ran anxiously to help him; but by good fortune he had fallen into a bush, in which he now lay.

It was now our turn to laugh; but we were not yet quite sure that he was unhurt, and as we knew not when or where the next cloud might arise, we helped him quickly to jump up and hurry from the spot.

" What's to be done now? " said Peterkin sadly.

" Make a fire, my boy, and dry ourselves," replied Jack.

" And here is material ready to our hand," said I, picking up a dry branch of a tree as we hurried up to the woods.

In about an hour after this, our clothes were again dry. While they were hanging up before the fire, we walked down to the beach, and soon observed that these strange clouds formed immediately after the fall of a huge wave, never before it; and that they did not form except when the wave was an extremely large one. From this we concluded that there must be an underground channel in the rock into which the water was driven by the larger waves, and finding no way of escape except through these small holes, was thus forced up through them. At any rate, we could not think of any other reason for these strange clouds, and this seemed a very simple and probable one.

A STRANGE FISH

" I say, Ralph, what's that in the water? Is it a shark? " said Jack, just as we were about to leave the place.

I immediately ran to the overhanging rock, from which he was looking down into the sea, and bent over it. There I saw a very faint pale object of a greenish colour, which seemed to move slightly while I looked at it.

" It's like a fish of some sort," said I.

" Hullo, Peterkin! " cried Jack. " Fetch your spear, here's work for it."

But when we tried to reach the object the spear was too short.

"A thick cloud of water burst upwards from a hole in the rock."

" There now," said Peterkin, " you were always telling me it was too long."

Jack now drove the spear hard towards the object, and let go his hold; but although it seemed to be well aimed, he must have missed, for the handle soon rose again; and when the spear was drawn up, there was the pale green object in exactly the same spot, slowly moving its tail.

" Very odd," said Jack.

But although it was certainly very odd, and though Jack and all of us drove the spear at it repeatedly, we could neither hit nor drive it away, so we were forced to continue our journey without discovering what it was. I wondered very much at this strange appearance in the water, and could not get it out of my mind for a long time afterwards. However, I quieted myself by making up my mind that I would pay a visit to it again at some other time.

CHAPTER 9

THE SECOND DAY OF OUR JOURNEY

OUR examination of the little valley proved to be most helpful. We found in it not only the same trees as we had already seen in our own valley, but also one or two others of a different kind. We had also the pleasure of discovering a strange vegetable, which Jack thought must certainly be that of which we had read as being among the South Sea Islands, and which was named taro. Also we found a large supply of yams, and another root like a potato in appearance. These were all quite new to us. We each put one of these roots in our pocket, intending to use them for our supper; of which more later. We also saw many beautiful birds here, and traces of some fourfooted animals again.

In the meantime the sun began to descend, so we returned to the shore, and pushed on round the cloud-producing rocks into the next valley. This was that valley of which I have spoken as running across the entire island. It was by far the largest and most beautiful that we had yet looked upon. Here were trees of every shape and size and colour which it is possible to think of, many of which we had not seen in the other valleys; for, the stream in this valley being larger, and the earth much richer than in the Valley of the Ship, it was clothed with a thicker growth of trees and plants.

Some trees were dark shining green, others of a rich and warm colour, pleasantly different from those of a pale light green, which were everywhere common. Among these we saw the broad dark heads of the bread-fruit, with its golden fruit; the pure, silvery leaves of the tree bearing the nuts from which we obtained our light, and several kinds which were very like the pine; while here and there, in groups and in single trees, rose the tall forms of the coconut palms, waving their graceful leaves high above all the rest.

NEW TREES

Now, while we were gazing round us in silent admiration, Jack uttered a cry of surprise, and pointing to an object a little to one side of us, said:

" That's a banyan tree."

" And what's a banyan tree? " asked Peterkin, as we walked towards it.

" A very strange one, as you shall see presently," replied Jack. " There is a wonderful thing about it. What a big one it is, to be sure! "

" *It!* " repeated Peterkin. " Why, there are dozens of banyans here! What do you mean by talking bad English? Is your sense deserting you, Jack? "

" There is but one tree here of this kind," replied Jack, " as you will see if you examine it."

And, sure enough, we did find that what we had supposed was a forest of trees was really only one. Its bark was of a light colour, and had a shining appearance, the leaves being spear-shaped, small, and of a beautiful green. But the wonderful thing about it was, that the branches, which grew out from the trunk like the arms of a cross, sent down long shoots to the ground, which, taking root, had themselves become trees, and were covered with bark like the tree itself. Many of these shoots had descended from the branches at various distances, and some of them were so large and strong that it was not easy at first to tell the child from the parent trunk. The shoots were of all sizes and in all conditions of growth, from the trunks we have just mentioned to small ropes which hung down and were about to take root, and thin brown threads still far from the ground, which waved about with every motion of the wind.

In short, it seemed to us that, if there were only space enough for it, this single tree would at length cover the whole island.

Shortly after this we came upon another strange tree, which, as its interesting shape afterwards proved extremely useful to us, must be described. Its proper name Jack did not know. However, there were quantities of fine nuts upon it, some of which we put in our pockets. But its trunk was the wonderful part of it. It rose to about twelve feet without a branch, and was not of great thickness—far from it, it was very thin for the size of the tree—but, to make up for this, there were four or five wonderful outgrowths in this trunk. These I cannot better describe than by asking the reader to suppose that five boards of two inches thick and three feet broad had been placed round the trunk of the tree, with their *edges* closely fixed to it, from the ground up to the branches, and that these boards had been covered over with the bark of the tree, and had become one with it. Without them the trunk could not have supported its heavy and leafy top. We found very many of these nut trees.

They grew chiefly on the banks of the stream, and were of all sizes.

While we were examining a small tree of this kind, Jack cut off a piece of a board with his axe, and found the wood to be firm and easily cut. Then he struck his axe into it with all his force, and very soon cut it off, close to the tree, first, however, having cut it across above and below. By this means he satisfied himself that we could now obtain short boards, as it were already cut, of any size and thickness that we desired; which was a very great discovery indeed—perhaps the most important we had yet made.

We now made our way back to the coast, intending to camp near the beach, as we found that the mosquitoes were a trouble in the forest. On our way we could not help admiring the birds which flew and called all round us. The colours of many of these birds were extremely bright—bright green, blue, and red being the common colours. We tried several times throughout the day to bring down one of these, both with the bow and the sling—not for mere sport, but to find out whether they were good for food. But we always missed, although once or twice we were very near hitting. As evening drew on, however, a flock of birds flew over. I sent a stone into the middle of them, and had the good fortune to kill one of them.

We were surprised, soon after, by a loud whistling noise above our heads; and on looking up, saw a flock of wild ducks flying towards the coast. We watched these, and observing where they came down, followed them up until we came upon a most lovely blue lake, not more than two hundred yards long, circled by green trees. Its smooth surface, in which we could see every leaf and branch quite clearly, was covered with various kinds of wild ducks, feeding among the rushes and broad-leaved water-plants which floated on it; while many other water-birds ran up and down most busily on its edge. These all flew quickly away the instant we made our appearance. While walking along the edge we observed fish in the water, but of what sort we could not tell.

Now, as we neared the shore, Jack and I said we would go a little out of our way to see if we could not get one of those ducks; so, directing Peterkin to go straight to the shore and make a fire, we separated, promising to join him again soon. But we did not find the ducks, although we made a careful search for half an hour. We were about to make our way back, when we came across one of the strangest sights that we had yet beheld.

THE PIGS

Just in front of us, at a distance of about ten yards, grew a fine tree, which certainly was the largest we had yet seen on the island. Its trunk was at least five feet round, with a smooth grey bark; above this the spreading branches were clothed with light green leaves, among which were groups of bright yellow fruit--so many as to bend down the branches with their great weight. This fruit was about the size of an orange. The ground at the foot of this tree was thickly covered with the fallen fruit, in the middle of which lay sleeping at least twenty pigs, of all ages and sizes, having quite filled themselves up with the fruit.

Jack and I could scarce hold in our laughter as we gazed at these fat, ugly animals, while they lay breathing heavily among the remains of their supper.

" Now, Ralph," said Jack, in a low whisper, " put a stone in your sling—a good big one—and shoot at that fat fellow with his back towards you. I'll try to put an arrow into that little pig over there."

" Don't you think we had better wake them up first? " I whispered. " It seems cruel to kill them while asleep."

" If I wanted sport, Ralph, I would certainly wake them up; but as we only want *meat*, we'll let them lie. Besides, we are not sure of killing them, so shoot away."

At these words, I slung my stone with so good an aim that it hit against the pig's side as if against the head of a drum; but it had no other effect than to make the animal start to its feet with a frightful cry of surprise, and rush away. At the same instant Jack shot, and the arrow pinned the little pig to the ground by the ear.

" I've missed, after all! " cried Jack, running forward with raised axe, while the little pig uttered a loud cry, tore the arrow from the ground, and ran away with it, along with the whole herd, into the bushes and disappeared, though we heard the noise they made long afterwards in the distance.

" That's a pity, now," said Jack, rubbing the point of his nose.

" Very," I replied, stroking mine.

" Well, we must make haste and get back to Peterkin," said Jack. " It's getting late." And without further words we threaded our way quickly through the woods to the shore.

When we reached it, we found wood laid out, the fire lighted and beginning to burn up, with other signs of preparation for our camp, but Peterkin was not to be found. We wondered very much at this, but Jack said that he might have gone to fetch water, so he gave a shout to let him know that we had arrived, and sat down upon a rock, while I threw off my coat and seized the axe, intending to split up one or two pieces of wood. But I had scarcely moved from the spot when, in the distance, we heard a most frightening shout, which was followed up by a burst of cries from the pigs, and a loud hurrah.

" I do believe," said I, " that Peterkin has met with the pigs."

" Hurrah! " shouted Peterkin in the distance.

We turned hastily towards the direction from which the sound came, and soon saw Peterkin walking along the beach towards us with a little pig stuck on the end of his long spear.

" Well done, my boy! " cried Jack, hitting him on the shoulder when he came up. " You're the best shot among us."

" Look here, Jack! " said Peterkin, as he took the animal from his spear. " Have you seen that hole," said he, pointing to the pig's ear; " and are you familiar with this arrow, eh? "

" Well, I declare! " said Jack.

" Of course you do," said Peterkin; " but pray stop declaring this time, for I'm very hungry, I can tell you; and it's a serious thing to charge a whole herd of pigs with their huge mother leading them."

SUPPER

We now began to prepare supper; and, truly, a good show of food we made, when all was laid out on a flat rock in the light of the blazing fire. There was, first of all, the little pig; then there was the taro root, and the yam, and the potato, and lastly, the bird.

We found great difficulty in making up our minds how we were to cook the pig. None of us had ever cut up one before, and we did not know exactly how to begin; besides, we had nothing but the axe to do it with, our knife having been forgotten. At last Jack jumped up and said:

" Don't let us waste more time talking about it, boys. Hold it up, Peterkin. There, lay the back leg on this piece of wood— so "; and he cut it off with a large portion of the body at a single blow of the axe. " Now the other—that's it." And having thus cut off the two back legs, he made several cuts in them, pushed a sharp pointed stick through each, and put them up before the blaze to roast. The bird was then cut open, washed clean in salt water, and treated in the same way. While these were cooking, we made a hole in the sand under the fire, into which we put our vegetables and covered them up.

The taro root was egg-shaped, about ten inches long and four or five thick. It was of a grey colour, and had a thick skin. We found it somewhat like an Irish potato, and very good. The yam was roundish, and had a rough brown skin. It was very sweet and tasted nice. The potato, we were surprised to find, was quite sweet and very good, as also were the pig and the bird too, when we came to taste them.

In fact this was decidedly the best supper we had enjoyed for many a day; and Jack said it was very much better than we ever got on board ship; and Peterkin said he feared that if we should remain long on the island he would think of nothing but eating; at which Jack replied that he need not fear that, for he did so already! And so, having eaten our fill, we laid ourselves comfortably down to sleep, upon a bed of branches under a coral rock.

CHAPTER 10

BACK TO OUR HOUSE

WHEN we awakened on the following morning, we found that the sun was already quite high in the sky, so I became sure that a heavy supper does not help one to rise early. However, we felt very strong and well, and very ready to have our breakfast. First, however, as was our custom, we had our morning swim.

We had not advanced on our journey much above a mile or so, when, on turning a point that showed us a new and beautiful group of islands, we were suddenly stopped by the frightful cry which had so alarmed us a few nights before. But this time we were by no means so much alarmed as on the occasion before, because at that time it was night, and now it was day; and I have always found, though I am unable to account for it, that daylight sends away many of the fears that attack us in the dark.

On hearing the sound, Peterkin hastily levelled his spear. " Now, what can it be? " said he, looking round at Jack. " I'll tell you what it is; if we are going to be kept in a constant condition of fear and surprise, as we have been for the last week, the sooner we're out of this island the better, in spite of the yams and coconuts and pigs and potatoes! "

As Peterkin said this, we heard the cry again, louder than before.

" It comes from one of these islands," said Jack.

" It must be a ghost, then," said Peterkin, " for I never heard any living thing make a noise like that."

We all turned our eyes towards the group of islands, where, on the largest, we observed strange objects moving on the shore.

" Soldiers they are—that's a fact! " cried Peterkin; gazing at them in the greatest surprise.

And, in truth, what Peterkin said seemed to me to be correct, for, at the distance from which we saw them, they appeared to be an army. There they stood, in ranks, in lines and in squares, with blue coats and white trousers. While we were looking at them, the dreadful cry came again over the water, and Peterkin said that he thought it must be an army sent out to kill the natives. At this Jack laughed, and said:

" Why, Peterkin, they are penguins! "

" Penguins? " repeated Peterkin.

" Yes, penguins, Peterkin, penguins—nothing more or less than big sea-birds, as you shall see one of these days, when we pay them a visit in our boat, which I mean to set about building the moment we get back to our house."

" So, then, our dreadful shouting ghosts, and our blood-thirsty soldiers," said Peterkin, " have changed to penguins—big sea-birds! Very good. Then I say that we should continue our journey as fast as possible, or our island will be turned into a dream before we get completely round it."

Now, as we continued on our way, I thought much over this new discovery and the strange appearance of these birds, of which Jack could only give us a very slight account; and I began to long to begin our boat, in order that we might go and look at them more narrowly. But by degrees these thoughts left me, and I began to be much taken up again with the interesting character of the country which we were passing through.

NEARING HOME

The second night we passed in much the same manner as the first, at about two-thirds of the way round the island, as we thought, and we hoped to sleep on the night following at our house. I will not here note so particularly all that we said and saw during the course of this second day, as we did not make any further important discoveries. The shore along which we travelled, and the various parts of the woods through which we passed, were very like those which have already been treated of. There were one or two observations that we made, however, and these were as follows:

We saw that, while many of the large fruit-bearing trees grew only in the valleys, and some of them only near the banks of the streams, where the soil was especially rich, the coconut palm grew everywhere; not only on the hill-sides, but also on the seashore, and even, as has been already said, on the coral reef itself, where the soil, if we may use the name, was nothing better than loose sand mixed with broken shells and coral rock. So near the sea, too, did this useful tree grow, that in many cases its roots were washed by the water from the waves. Yet we found the trees growing thus on the sands to be quite as fine as those growing in the valleys, and the fruit as good, also.

We found several more herds of pigs in the woods, but we did not kill any of them, having more than enough for our present needs. We saw, also, many of their footmarks in this district.

During the rest of the day we pursued our journey, and examined the other end of the large valley, which we found to be so much like the parts already described, that I shall not say anything about what we saw in this place. We arrived at our house in the evening, and found everything just in the same condition as we had left it three days before.

When we lay down that night under the shelter of the house, we fell immediately into very deep sleep. I am quite sure about this, for Jack afterwards admitted the fact, and Peterkin, although he denied it, I heard breathing loudly in his sleep two minutes after lying down. In this condition we remained all night and the whole of the following day without awakening once, or so much as moving our places. When we did awake it was near sunset, and we merely rose to swallow some food. As Peterkin said, we took breakfast at tea-time, and then went to bed again, where we lay till the following morning.

After this we rose feeling very wide awake, but much alarmed for fear that we had lost count of a day. However, on considering the subject, we were all three of the same opinion as to how long we had slept, and so our minds were put at ease.

MY HOLE IN THE ROCK

For many days after this, while Peterkin and Jack were busily employed in building a little boat out of the natural boards of the nut tree, I spent much of my time in examining with the glass from the telescope the strange things that were constantly happening in my hole in the rock. Here I saw those strange animals which stick, like little red, yellow, and green masses, to the rocks, put forth, as it were, many arms and wait till little fish or other small animals touch them. Then they instantly seize them, fold arm after arm around them, and so take them inside.

Here I saw the ceaseless working of those little coral animals whose efforts have built up vast rocks and huge reefs round the islands of the Pacific. And I observed that many of these animals, though extremely small, were very beautiful, coming out of their holes in a circle of fine threads. Here I saw strange little shell-fish opening a hole in their backs and putting out a thin, feathery hand, with which, I doubt not, they dragged their food into their mouths. Here, also, I saw those crabs which have shells only in the front of their bodies, but no shell whatever on their very tender tails, so that, in order to protect them, they thrust them into the empty shells of some other shell-fish, and when they grow too big for one, change into another. But, most strange of all, I saw an animal which had the wonderful power, when it became ill, of casting its inside and its teeth away from it, and getting an entirely new set in the course of a few months! All this I saw, and a great deal more, by means of my hole in the rock and my glass; but I will not set down more particulars here, as I have still much to tell of what happened to us while we remained on this island.

CHAPTER II

DIAMOND CAVE

" Come, Jack," cried Peterkin, one morning about three weeks after we had come back from our long journey, " let's be cheerful to-day, and do something at which we can run about. I'm quite tired of hammering and bammering, cutting and butting at that little boat of ours, that seems as hard to build as Noah's. Let us go to the mountain-top, or have a hunt after the wild ducks, or make a dash at the pigs. I'm quite flat—flat as a board; in fact, I want something to toss me up, as it were. Eh! what do you say to it? "

" Well," answered Jack, throwing down the axe with which he was just about to proceed towards the boat, " if that's what you want, I would advise you to make a journey to the cloud-making rocks. The last one we had to do with tossed you up a fine height; perhaps the next will send you higher, who knows, if you're at all reasonable in what you expect! "

" Jack, my dear boy," said Peterkin gravely, " you are really becoming too fond of fun. It's a thing I don't at all approve of, and if you don't give it up, I fear that, for the good of both of us, we shall have to part."

" Well, then, Peterkin," replied Jack with a smile, "what would you have? "

" Have? " said Peterkin. " I would *have* nothing. I didn't say I wanted to *have;* I said that I wanted to *do*."

" By the way," said I, " I remember now that we have not yet discovered the nature of the appearance that we saw near the cloud-making rocks, on our journey round the island. Perhaps it would be well to go for that purpose."

" Humph! " cried Peterkin, " I know the nature of it well enough."

" What was it? " said I.

" It was of a *strange* nature, to be sure! " said he, with a wave of his hand, while he rose from the log on which he had been sitting and put on his belt, into which he pushed his huge stick.

" Well, then, let us away to the cloud-making rocks," cried Jack, going up to the house for his bow and arrows; " and bring your spear, Peterkin. It may be useful."

We now, having made up our minds to examine into this matter, set out eagerly in the direction of the cloud-making rocks, which, as I have before mentioned, were not far from the place where we were now living. On arriving there we hastened down to the edge of the rocks and gazed over into the sea, where we observed the pale-green object still easily to be seen, moving its tail slowly backwards and forwards in the water.

" Most strange! " said Jack.

" Very unusual! " said I.

" Takes the prize! " said Peterkin.

THE STRANGE FISH AGAIN

" Now, Jack," he added, " you made such a poor figure when you last tried to stick that object, that I would advise you to let me try it. If it has got a heart at all, I'll promise to send my spear right through the middle of it; if it hasn't got a heart, I'll send it through the spot where its heart ought to be."

" Go on then, my boy," replied Jack with a laugh.

Peterkin immediately took the spear, held it for a second or two above his head, then sent it like an arrow into the sea. Down it went straight into the centre of the green object, passed quite through it, and came up immediately afterwards, pure and unmarked, while the strange tail moved quietly as before!

" Now," said Peterkin gravely, " that animal is heartless; I'll have nothing more to do with it."

" I'm pretty sure now," said Jack, " that it is merely some form of light; but I must say I do not understand why it remains always in that exact spot."

I did not understand it either, and thought with Jack that it must be natural light, of which appearance we had seen much while on our way to these seas.

" But," said I, " there is nothing to stop us from diving down to it, now that we are sure it is not a shark."

" True," answered Jack, stripping off his clothes; " I'll go down, Ralph, as I'm better at diving than you are. Now then, Peterkin, out of the road! "

Jack stepped forward, joined his hands above his head, bent over the rocks, and dived into the sea. For a second or two the water thrown up by his dive hid him from view; then the water became calm, and we saw him swimming far down in the middle of the green object. Suddenly he went below it, and disappeared completely from our sight! We gazed anxiously down at the spot where he had disappeared for nearly a minute, expecting every moment to see him rise again for breath; but fully a minute passed, and still he did not appear again. Two minutes passed! and then a flood of alarm rushed in upon my soul, when I considered that, during all the time I had known him, Jack had never remained under water more than a minute at a time; indeed, not often so long.

JACK DISAPPEARS

" Oh, Peterkin! " I said, in a voice that trembled with increasing fear, " something has happened. It is more than three minutes now."

But Peterkin did not answer, and I observed that he was gazing down into the water with a look of great fear, while his face was overspread with a deadly paleness. Suddenly he jumped to his feet, and rushed about in a dreadful state, crying, " Oh, Jack, Jack! He is gone! It must have been a shark, and he is gone for ever! "

For the next five minutes I know not what I did; the depth of my feelings almost took away my senses. But I was recalled to myself by Peterkin seizing me by the shoulder and gazing wildly into my face, while he exclaimed:

" Ralph! Ralph! perhaps he has only fainted. Dive for him, Ralph! "

It seemed strange that this did not occur to me before. In a moment I rushed to the edge of the rocks, and, without waiting to throw off my garments, was on the point to spring into the waves, when I observed something black rising up through the green object. In another moment Jack's head rose to the surface, and he gave a wild shout, throwing back the water from his hair, as he always did after a dive. Now we were almost as much surprised at seeing him appear, well and strong, as we had been at first at his non-appearance. To the best of our judgment, he had been nearly ten minutes under water, perhaps longer, and it required no effort of our reason to make known to us that this was utterly impossible for mortal man to do and keep his strength and senses. It was therefore with a strange feeling that I held down my hand and assisted him to climb up the steep rocks. But no such feeling came over Peterkin. When Jack gained the rocks and sat himself on one, breathing deeply, he threw his arms round his neck and burst into a flood of tears.

" Oh, Jack, Jack! " said he. " Where were you? What kept you so long? "

After a few moments Peterkin became calm enough to sit still and listen to Jack's explanation.

THE MYSTERY EXPLAINED

" Now, lads," said Jack, " that green object is not a shark; it is a stream of light issuing from a cave in the rocks. Just after I made my dive, I observed that this light came from the side of the rock above which we are now sitting; so I swam towards it, and saw an opening into some place or other that appeared to be light within. For one instant I stopped to think whether I ought to go in. Then I made up my mind, and dashed into it. For you see, Peterkin, although I take some time to tell this, it happened in the space of a few seconds, so that I knew I had wind enough in me to serve to bring me out of the hole and up to the surface again.

" Well, I was just on the point of turning—for I began to feel a little uncomfortable in such a place—when it seemed to me as if there was a faint light right above me. I swam upwards, and found my head out of water. This pleased me greatly, for I now felt that I could take in air enough to allow me to return the way I came. Then it all at once occurred to me that I might not be able to find the way out again; but, on glancing downwards, my mind was put quite at rest by seeing the green light below me streaming into the cave, just like the light that we had seen streaming out of it, only what I now saw was much brighter.

EXPLORING THE CAVE

" At first I could scarcely see anything as I gazed round me, it was so dark; but after a time my eyes became used to it, and

I found that I was in a huge cave, part of the walls of which I observed on each side of me. The roof just above me was also to be seen, and I fancied that I could see beautiful shining objects there; but the farther end of the cave was in darkness. While I was looking round me in great wonder, it came into my head that you two would think I was drowned; so I dived down again in a great hurry, rose to the surface, and—here I am! "

When Jack ended his story of what he had seen in this cave, I could not rest satisfied till I had dived down to see it; which I did, but found it so dark, as Jack had said, that I could scarcely see anything. When I came back, we had a long talk about it, during which I observed that Peterkin had a most sad expression on his face.

" What's the matter, Peterkin? " said I.

" The matter? " he replied. " It's all very well for you two to be talking away like fishes about the wonders of this cave, but you know I must be content to hear about it, while you are enjoying yourselves down there like mad sharks. It's really too bad."

" I'm very sorry for you, Peterkin, indeed I am," said Jack, " but we cannot help you. If you would only learn to dive——"

" Learn to fly, you might as well say! " answered Peterkin, in a very cross tone.

We both laughed and shook our heads, for it was clear that nothing was to be made of Peterkin in the water. But we could not rest satisfied till we had seen more of this cave; so, after further talk, Jack and I determined to try if we could take down a stick with us, and set fire to it in the cave.

This we found to be very difficult, but we did it at last by the following means: First, we took the bark of a certain tree, which we cut into strips, and fastened together with a kind of gum, which we also obtained from another tree; neither of which trees, however, was known by name to Jack. This, when prepared, we wrapped up in a great number of pieces of coconut cloth, so that we were sure it could not get wet during the short time it should be under water. Then we rolled up some dry grass and a few small pieces of wood, which, with a little bow and drill like those described before, we wrapped up in coconut cloth. When all was ready we laid aside our garments, with the exception of our trousers, which, as we did not know what rough climbing on rocks we might be subjected to, we kept on.

Then we advanced to the edge of the rocks, Jack carrying one bundle, with the stick, I the other, with the things for producing fire.

" Now don't weary for us, Peterkin, should we be gone some time," said Jack; " we'll be sure to come back in half an hour at the very latest, however interesting the cave should be, that we may ease your mind."

" Farewell! " said Peterkin, coming up to us with a look of deep but unreal sadness, while he shook hands and kissed each of us on the cheek. " Farewell! And while you are gone I shall rest my weary limbs under the shelter of this bush, and think of the changefulness of all things earthly, and especially of the condition of a poor sailor boy! "

So saying, Peterkin waved his hand, turned from us, and cast himself upon the ground with a look of great sadness, which was so well done that I almost thought it real. We both laughed, and, springing from the rocks together, dived head first into the sea.

THE CAVE

We gained the inside of the underwater cave without difficulty, and, on coming out from the waves, supported ourselves for some time by treading-water, while we held the two bundles above our heads. This we did in order to let our eyes become used to the darkness. Then, when we could see enough, we swam to a rock, and landed in safety. Having got the water out of our trousers, and dried ourselves as well as we could, we proceeded to light the stick. This we did without difficulty in a few minutes; and no sooner did it burn up than we were struck speechless with the wonderful objects that were shown to our gaze.

The roof of the cave just above us seemed to be about ten feet high, but grew higher as it went back into the distance, until it was lost in darkness. It seemed to be made of coral, and was supported by great columns of the same material. Huge spear-shaped masses (as they appeared to us) hung from it in various places. These, however, were formed of a kind of coral, which seemed to flow in a watery form towards the point of each, where it became rock. A good many drops fell, however, to the rock below, and these formed little points, which rose to meet the points above. Some of them had already met, and thus we saw how the columns were formed, which at first seemed to us as if they had been placed there by some human builder to support the roof.

As we advanced farther in, we saw that the floor was made of the same material as the columns; and it presented the strange appearance of little waves, such as are formed on water when gently blown upon by the wind. There were several openings on either hand in the walls, that seemed to lead into other caves; but these we did not go into at this time. We also observed that the roof was strangely marked in many places, as if it were a noble church; and the walls, as well as the roof, shone in the light, and threw back flashes, as if they were covered with precious stones.

Although we proceeded far into this cave, we did not come to the end of it, and we were obliged to return more speedily than we would have liked to have done, as our stick was nearly burnt down. We did not observe any openings in the roof, or any signs of places whereby light might enter; but near the entrance to the cave stood a huge mass of pure white coral rock, which caught and threw back the little light that found an entrance through the cave's mouth, and thus produced, we thought, the pale-green object which had first drawn our attention to the

"*We observed that the rock was strangely marked in many places.*"

place. We thought, also, that the light-turning power of this rock was that which gave forth the light that faintly lit up the first part of the cave.

Before diving through the entrance again we put out the small piece of our stick that remained, and left it in a dry spot; thinking that we might possibly need it, if at any future time we should chance to wet our stick for lighting us while diving into the cave. As we stood for a few minutes after it was out, waiting till our eyes became accustomed to the darkness, we could not help remarking the deep quiet and the unearthly darkness of all around us.

" Now, Ralph, are you ready? " said Jack, in a low voice that seemed to echo up into the roof above.

" Quite ready."

" Come along, then," said he; and diving off the rock into the water, we swam through the narrow entrance. In a few seconds we were on the rocks above, and receiving the welcome of our friend Peterkin.

CHAPTER 12

PIG STICKING

It was pleasant to us to breathe the pure air and to enjoy the glad sunshine after our long walk in the Diamond Cave, as we named it; for although we did not stop more than half an hour away, it seemed to us much longer. While we were dressing, and during our walk home, we did our best to satisfy poor Peterkin, who seemed very sorry that he could not dive. There was no help for it, however.

After having told all we could to Peterkin about the Diamond

Cave, we were making our way rapidly homewards when a well-
known sound came to our ears.

" That's the ticket! " was Peterkin's strange cry, as he started
up and lifted his spear.

" Listen! " cried Jack. " These are your friends, Peterkin.
They must have come over on purpose to pay you a friendly
visit, for it is the first time we have seen them on this side the
island."

" Come along! " cried Peterkin, hurrying towards the wood,
while Jack and I followed, smiling.

More noises, much louder than before, came down the valley.
At this time we were just opposite the small valley which lay
between the Valley of the Ship and Diamond Cave.

" I say, Peterkin," cried Jack, in a whisper.

" Well, what is't? "

" Stop a bit, man. These pigs are just up there on the hill-side.
If you go and stand with Ralph under that rock, I'll run round
behind and drive them through the valley, so that you'll have a
better chance of picking out a good one. Now, mind you get a
fat young pig, Peterkin," added Jack, as he jumped into the
bushes.

" Won't I just! " said Peterkin, licking his lips, as we took our
station beside the rock. " I feel quite a tender liking for young
pigs in my heart. Perhaps it would be more correct to say in
my——"

" There they come! " cried I, as a loud shout from Jack sent
the whole herd down the hill. Now Peterkin, being unable to
keep still, crept a short way up a very steep grassy hill, in order
to get a better view of the pigs before they came up; and just as
he raised his head above its top, two little pigs, which had run
faster than their companions, rushed over the top with the ut-
most haste. One of these brushed close past Peterkin's ear; the
other, unable to stop its flight, went, as Peterkin himself afterwards expressed it, " bash " into his arms with a sudden cry,
which was caused more by the force of the blow than the will of

the animal, and both of them rolled down to the foot of the hill. No sooner was this reached than the little pig recovered its feet, threw up its tail, and ran crying from the spot. But I sent a large stone after it, which, being fortunately well aimed, hit it behind the ear, and brought it to the earth.

" Fine, Ralph! That's your sort! " cried Peterkin, who, to my surprise and great joy, had risen to his feet unhurt, though covered with earth.

He rushed madly towards the valley, which the cries of the pigs told us they were now approaching. I had made up my mind that I would not kill another, as, if Peterkin should be successful, two were more than enough for our wants at the present time. Suddenly they all burst forth—two or three little ones in advance, and a huge old pig with a herd of little ones at her heels.

" Now, Peterkin," said I, " there's a nice little fat one; just spear it."

PETERKIN MAKES SHOES

But Peterkin did not move; he allowed it to pass unharmed. I looked at him in surprise, and saw that his lips were closed and his eyebrows bent, as if he were about to fight with some awful enemy.

" What is it? " I asked, with some fear.

Suddenly he lifted his spear, ran forward, and, with a shout that nearly froze my blood, speared the old pig to the heart. Indeed, the spear went in at one side and came out at the other!

" Oh, Peterkin! " said I, going up to him. " What have you done? "

" Done? I've killed their mother, that's all," said he, looking with a somewhat fearful expression at the dead animal.

" Hallo! What's this? " said Jack, as he came up. " Why, Peterkin, you must be fond of hard meat. If you mean to eat this old pig, she'll try your teeth, I fancy. What made you stick *her*, Peterkin? "

" Why, the fact is I want a pair of shoes."

" What have your shoes to do with the old pig? " said I, smiling.

" My present shoes have certainly nothing to do with her," replied Peterkin; " but she will have a good deal to do with my future shoes. The fact is, when I saw you hit that pig so well, Ralph, it struck me that there was little use in killing another. Then I remembered all at once that I had long wanted some leather to make shoes of, and this old mother seemed so hard that I just made up my mind to stick her, and you see I've done it! "

" That you certainly have, Peterkin," said Jack, as he was examining the animal.

We now considered how we were to carry our meat home, for, although the distance was short, the pig was very heavy. At length we hit on the plan of tying its four feet together, and passing the spear handle between them. Jack took one end on his shoulder, I took the other on mine, and Peterkin carried the small pig.

Thus we came back to our house, bearing, as Peterkin said, the fruits of a noble hunt. As he afterwards spoke in the same warm terms of the supper that followed, there is every reason to believe that we retired that night to our leafy beds in a high state of satisfaction.

CHAPTER 13

WE BUILD A BOAT

FOR many days after this Jack applied himself to the making of our boat, which at length began to look somewhat like one. But those only who hav, had the thing to do can have a right idea of the difficulty of such a work, with no other tools than an axe, a bit of iron, a sail-needle, and a broken knife. But Jack did it.

As this boat was interesting in its way, a few words here about the manner of its building may not be out of place.

I have already mentioned the tree with its wonderful boards. This tree, then, furnished us with the chief part of our material. First of all, Jack sought out a limb of a tree of such a form and size as, while it should form the bottom, a bend at either end should form the back and front posts. Such a piece, however, was not easy to obtain; but at last he got it, by rooting up a small tree which had a branch growing in the proper direction about ten feet up its stem, with two strong roots growing in such a form as enabled him to make a boat flat at the back. This placed, he took three branching roots, which he fitted to the bottom at equal distances, thus forming three strong supports.

Now the squaring and shaping of the roots, and the cutting of the places for them in the bottom was an easy enough matter, as it was all work for the axe, in the use of which Jack was become wonderfully good; but it was quite a different affair when he came to nailing the supports to the bottom, for we had no tool for boring a large hole, and no nails to fasten them with. We were, indeed, almost stopped here; but Jack at length made a tool that served very well. Two holes were bored in each support, about an inch and a half apart, and also down into the bottom, but not quite through. Into these were placed strong pieces of wood from a tree called iron-wood; and, when they were hammered well home, the supports were as firmly fixed as if they had been nailed with iron. But, besides the wooden nails, the sides were firmly tied to the end posts and supports by means of a kind of rope which we had made out of the coconut cloth. When a number of the threads were joined together they formed excellent rope. At first we tied the different lengths together; but afterwards we managed to make good rope of any size or length we chose. Of course it cost us much time and labour, but Jack kept up our spirits when we grew weary, and so all that we required was at last made.

Boards were now cut off the trees of about an inch thick. These were dressed with the axe—but roughly, for an axe is ill fitted for such work. Five of these boards on each side were enough; and we formed the boat in a very rounded shape, in order to have as little turning of the boards as possible, for although we could easily bend them, we could not easily turn them. Having no nails to fix the boards with, we threw aside the ordinary fashion of boat-building and made up one of our own. The boards were therefore placed on each other's edges, and sewn together with the rope already mentioned. They were also thus sewed to the front, the back, and the bottom.

Besides this, we placed between the edges of the boards coconut cloth, which, as it swelled when wetted, would, we hoped, make our little vessel watertight. Thus the inside was covered with a watertight material; while the outside, being uncovered so that the water would make it swell, was, we hoped, likely to keep the boat quite dry. I may add that our hopes were not vain ones.

OUR FOOD

While Jack was thus at work, Peterkin and I sometimes assisted him; but as our assistance was not much required, we more frequently went a-hunting on the wide mud-flats at the entrance of the long valley which lay nearest to our house. Here we found large flocks of ducks of various kinds, some of them being so much like the wild ducks of our own country that I think they must have been the same. On these occasions we took the bow and the sling, with both of which we were often successful, though I must say I was the least so. Our suppers were thus pleasantly different from each other, and sometimes we had such a large choice spread out before us that we frequently knew not with which food to begin.

The large flat stone, or rock of coral, which stood just in front of the entrance to our house, was our table. On this rock we had spread out the few articles we possessed the day the ship struck; and on the same rock during many a day afterwards, we spread out the rich supply with which we had been blessed on our Coral Island. Sometimes we sat down at this table to a feast consisting of hot rolls—as Peterkin called the newly baked breadfruit—a roast pig, roast duck, boiled and roasted yams, coconuts, taro, and sweet potatoes; which we followed up with fruit.

Occasionally Peterkin tried to make some new dishes; but these generally turned out so bad that in the end he gave up his trials—not forgetting, however, to point out to Jack that his failure had proved the falseness of the saying which he, Jack, was constantly repeating—namely, that " where there's a will there's a way." For he had a great will to become a cook, but could by no means find a way to become one.

One day, while Peterkin and I were seated beside our table, on which dinner was spread, Jack came up from the beach, and, throwing down his axe, cried:

THE BOAT FINISHED

" There, my boys, the boat's finished at last, so we've nothing to do now but shape two pairs of oars, and then we may put to sea as soon as we like."

This piece of news threw us into a state of great joy; for although we knew that the boat had been slowly getting near its completion, it had taken so long that we did not expect it to be quite ready for at least two or three weeks. But Jack had worked hard and said nothing, in order to surprise us.

" My dear fellow," cried Peterkin, " you're a perfect angel. But why did you not tell us it was so nearly ready? Won't we have a fine sail to-morrow, eh? "

" Don't talk so much, Peterkin," said Jack; " and, pray, hand me a bit of that pig."

" Certainly, my dear," cried Peterkin, seizing the axe. " What part will you have? A leg, or a wing, or a piece off the body—which? "

" A hind leg, if you please," answered Jack; " and, pray, be so good as to include the tail."

" With all my heart," said Peterkin, exchanging the axe for his iron knife, with which he cut off the desired portion.

" Well, but," continued Peterkin, " I was talking of a sail to-morrow. Can't we have one, Jack? "

" No," replied Jack, " we can't have a sail, but I hope we shall have a row, as I intend to work hard at the oars this afternoon, and, if we can't get them finished by sunset, we'll light our nuts, and finish before we turn into bed."

" Very good," said Peterkin. " I'll help you, if I can."

" Afterwards," continued Jack, " we will make a sail out of the coconut cloth, and fix up a mast, and then we shall be able to sail to some of the other islands, and visit our old friends the penguins."

The idea of being so quickly able to visit the other islands and enjoy a sail over the beautiful sea gave us much delight, and after dinner we set about making the oars in good earnest. We worked hard and rapidly, so that when the sun went down, Jack and I came back to the house with four fine oars, which required little to be done to them save a slight shaping with the knife.

After supper we retired to rest and to dream of wonderful adventures in our little boat, and distant voyages upon the sea.

CHAPTER 14

WE EXAMINE THE LAGOON

IT was a bright, clear, beautiful morning, when we first put out our little boat and rowed out upon the calm waters of the lagoon. Not a breath of wind moved the surface of the sea. Not a cloud spotted the deep blue sky. The sea was shining like a sheet of glass, yet slowly rising and falling with the long deep swell that, all the world round, indicates the life of Ocean; and the bright seaweeds and corals were shining at the bottom of that clear water, as we rowed over it, like rare and precious gems.

At first, in the strength of our delight, we rowed without aim or object. But after the first joy of our spirits died down, we began to look about us and to consider what we should do.

" I vote that we row to the reef," cried Peterkin.

" And I vote that we visit the islands within the lagoon," said I.

" And I vote we do both," cried Jack, " so pull away, boys."

As I have already said, we had made four oars, but our boat was so small that only two were necessary. The second pair were kept in case anything should happen to the others. It was therefore only needful that two of us should row, while the third guided us, by means of an oar, and changed places with the rowers occasionally.

ON THE REEF

First we landed on one of the small islands, and ran all over it, but saw nothing worthy of particular notice. Then we landed on a larger island, on which were growing a few coconut trees. Not having eaten anything that morning, we gathered a few of the nuts and breakfasted. After this we pulled straight out to sea and landed on the coral reef.

This was indeed a new and interesting sight to us. We had now been so long on shore that we had almost forgotten the appearance of waves, for there were none within the lagoon. But now, all the joy of the sailor was awakened in our hearts, and as we gazed on the widespread ruin of that single huge wave that burst in thunder at our feet, we forgot the Coral Island behind us; we forgot our house and the calm rest of the quiet woods; we forgot all that had passed during the last few months, and remembered nothing but the storms, the calms, the fresh winds, and the ever moving waves of the open sea.

This huge, ceaseless wave, of which I have so often spoken, was a much larger and finer object than we had at all imagined it to be. It rose many yards above the level of the sea, and could be seen approaching at some distance from the reef. Slowly and calmly it came on, gaining greater volume and speed as it advanced, until it took the form of a clear watery arch, which glanced in the bright sun. On it came—the upper edge lipped gently over, and it fell with a roar that seemed as though the heart of Ocean were broken in the noise of the water, while the coral reef appeared to tremble beneath the mighty shock!

We gazed long and wonderingly at this great sight, and it was with difficulty we could tear ourselves away from it. As I have once before mentioned, this wave broke in many places over the reef, and scattered some of its water into the lagoon, but in most places the reef was broad enough and high enough to receive and check its entire force. In many places the coral rocks were covered with plants—the beginning, as it appeared to us, of future islands.

Thus, on this reef, we came to see how most of the small islands of those seas are formed. On one part we saw the water from the wave washing over the rocks, and millions of little busy creatures continuing the work of building up this living wall. At another place, which was just a little too high for the waves to wash over it, the coral animals were all dead; for we found that they never did their work above water. Again, in other spots the ceaseless waves of the sea had broken the dead coral in pieces, and cast it up in the form of sand. Here sea-birds had come to earth, little pieces of seaweed and bits of wood had been washed up, seeds of plants had been carried by the wind, and a few lovely blades of bright green had already come up, which, when they died, would increase the size and richness of these gems of Ocean. At other places these little islands had grown greatly, and were shaded by one or two coconut trees, which grew in the sand, and were constantly washed by the water of the ocean.

Having satisfied and enjoyed ourselves during the whole day, in our little boat, we rowed back, somewhat wearied, and rather hungry, to our house.

" Now," said Jack, " as our boat serves us so well, we will get a mast and sail made immediately."

" So we will," cried Peterkin, as we all helped to drag the boat above high-water mark; " we'll light our light and set about it this very night. Hurrah, my boys, pull away! "

As we dragged our boat, we observed that she rubbed heavily on her bottom, and as the sands were in this place mixed with broken coral rocks, we saw portions of the wood being rubbed off.

" Hallo," cried Jack, on seeing this; " that won't do. The bottom will be worn off in no time at this rate."

" So it will," said I, thinking deeply as to how this might be stopped. But I could think of no way out save that of putting a plate of iron on the bottom; but as we had no iron, I knew not what was to be done. " It seems to me, Jack," I added, " that it is impossible to stop the bottom being worn off thus."

" Impossible! " cried Peterkin. " My dear Ralph, you are mistaken; there is nothing so easy."

" How? " I asked, in some surprise.

" Why, by not using the boat at all! " replied Peterkin.

WE MAKE A SAIL

" Be quiet, Peterkin," said Jack, as he shouldered the oars; " come along with me and I'll give you work to do. In the first place, you will go and collect coconut cloth, and set to work to make sewing thread with it——"

" Please, captain," cried Peterkin, " I've got lots of it made already—more than enough, as a little friend of mine used to be in the habit of saying every day after dinner."

" Very well," continued Jack; " then you'll help Ralph to get coconut cloth, and cut it into shape, after which we'll make a sail of it. I'll see to getting the mast and the ropes; so let's to work."

And to work we went right busily, so that in three days from that time we had set up a mast and sail, with the necessary ropes, in our little boat. The sail was not, indeed, very handsome to look at, as it was formed of a number of pieces of cloth; but we had sewed it well by means of our sailneedle, so that it was strong, which was the chief thing.

Jack had also overcome the difficulty about the bottom, by pinning to it a *false* bottom. This was a piece of wood as long and as wide as the real bottom, and about five inches deep. He made it of this thickness because the boat would be thereby made not only much more safe, but more able to make its way against the wind; which, in a sea where the strong winds blow so long and so hard in one direction, was a matter of great importance. This piece of wood was fixed very firmly to the bottom; and we now put our boat into the water with the comfort of knowing that when the false bottom should be worn off we could easily put on another; but, should the real bottom have been worn away, we could not have put on another without taking our boat to pieces.

The mast and sail served us excellently, and we now sailed about in the lagoon with great delight, and examined with much interest the appearance of our island from a distance. Also, we gazed into the water, and watched for hours the strange and bright-coloured fish among the corals and seaweed. Peterkin also made a fishing-line, and Jack made a number of hooks, some of which were very good, others very bad. Some of these hooks were made of iron-wood, which did pretty well, the wood being extremely hard, and Jack made them very thick and large. Some of the bones in fish-heads also served this purpose pretty well. But that which formed our best and most serviceable hook was the brass finger-ring belonging to Jack.

It would be a matter of much time and labour to describe the appearance of the many fish that were day after day drawn into our boat by means of the brass hook. Peterkin always caught them —for we observed that he obtained much pleasure from fishing—while Jack and I found enough to interest us in looking on, also in gazing down at the coral groves.

During these delightful fishing and boating journeys we caught many fish, which we found to be very good to eat. Moreover, we discovered many shell-fish, so that we had no lack of change in our food; and, indeed, we never passed a week without making some new and interesting discovery of some sort or other, either on the land or in the sea.

"We now sailed about in the lagoon."

CHAPTER 15

PENGUIN ISLAND

ONE day, not long after our little boat was finished, we were sitting on the rocks above Diamond Cave, and talking of a journey which we intended to make to Penguin Island the next day.

"You see," said Peterkin, "it might be all very well for a fellow like me to remain here and leave the penguins alone, but it would be quite against your characters as clever fellows to remain any longer without knowing the customs of these birds, so the quicker we go the better."

"Very true," said I; "there is nothing I desire so much as to have a closer view of them."

"And I think," said Jack, "that you had better remain at home, Peterkin."

"Stay at home!" cried Peterkin. "My dear fellow, you would certainly lose your way, or turn the boat over, if I were not there to take care of you."

"Ah, true," said Jack gravely; "that did not occur to me; no doubt you must go. Our boat does require a good deal of weight; and all that you say, Peterkin, carries so much weight with it, that we won't need stones if you go."

We prepared a supply of food, for we intended to be away at least a night or two, perhaps longer. This took us some time to do, for while Jack was busy with the boat, Peterkin was sent into the woods to spear a pig or two, and had to search long, sometimes, before he found them. Peterkin was usually sent when we wanted a pig (which was often), because he could run so wonderfully fast that he found no difficulty in catching the pigs; but being dreadfully careless, he almost always fell over stones in the course of his wild chase, and usually came home with the skin off his legs. But although Peterkin was often unfortunate in the way of getting falls, he was successful on the present occasion in hunting, and came back before evening with three very nice little pigs.

I also was successful in my visit to the mudflats, where I killed several ducks. So that, when we loaded our boat at sunrise the following morning, we found our store of food to be more than enough. We thought that this supply would last us for several days; but we afterwards found that it was much more than we required, especially in regard to the coconuts, of which we found large supplies wherever we went. However, as Peterkin said, it was better to have too much than too little, as we knew not what we might meet during our journey.

WE SET OUT

It was a very calm, sunny morning when we set forth and rowed over the lagoon towards the opening in the reef, and passed between the two green islands that guard the entrance. We met with some difficulty and no little danger in passing the big waves at the reef, and shipped a good deal of water; but, once past the wave, we found ourselves floating calmly on the long oily swell that rose and fell slowly as it rolled over the wide ocean.

Penguin Island lay on the other side of our own island, at about a mile beyond the outer reef, and we thought that it must be at least twenty miles distant by the way we should have to go. We might, indeed, have shortened the way by coasting round our island inside of the lagoon, and going out at the opening in the reef nearly opposite to Penguin Island; but we preferred to go by the open sea—first, because it was a bolder thing to do, and, secondly, because we should have the pleasure of again feeling the motion of the sea, which we all loved very much, not suffering from sea-sickness.

" I wish we had a wind," said Jack.

" So do I," cried Peterkin, resting on his oar and wiping his heated brow; " pulling is hard work. Oh dear, if we could only catch a hundred or two of these sea-birds, tie them to the boat with long strings, and make them fly as we want them, how fine it would be! "

" Or bore a hole through a shark's tail, and put a rope through it, eh? " remarked Jack. " But, I say, it seems that my wish is going to be granted, for here comes a wind. Ship your oar, Peterkin. Up with the mast, Ralph; I'll see to the sail. Look out for storms! "

This last speech was caused by the sudden appearance of a dark-blue line on the sky-line, which, in a short space of time, swept down on us, raising great waves as it went. We presented the back of the boat to its first force, and, in a few seconds, it calmed down into a good wind, before which we spread our sail and flew swiftly over the waves. Although the wind died away soon afterwards, it had been so stiff while it lasted that we were carried over the greater part of our way before it fell calm again; so that, when the noise of the sail against the mast told us that it was time to take up the oars again, we were not much more than a mile from Penguin Island.

" There go the soldiers! " cried Peterkin, as we came in sight of it. " How clean their white trousers look this morning! I wonder if they will receive us kindly. D'you think they are kind, Jack? "

" Don't talk, Peterkin, but pull away and you shall see shortly."

THE PENGUINS

As we drew near to the island we found much to laugh at in the movements and appearance of these strange birds. Having approached to within a few yards of the island, which was a low rock, with no other plants on it than a few bushes, we lay on our oars and gazed at the birds with surprise and pleasure, they returning our gaze with interest.

We now saw that their soldier-like appearance was owing to the stiff, erect manner in which they sat on their short legs— " bolt-upright," as Peterkin expressed it. They had black heads, long sharp beaks, white chests, and dark-blue backs. Their wings were very short, and we soon saw that they used them for the purpose of swimming under water. There were no proper feathers on these wings, but a sort of scales, which also thickly covered their bodies. Their legs were short, and placed so far back that the birds, while on land, were obliged to stand up straight in order to keep their balance; but in the water they floated like other water-birds. At first we were so surprised with the noise which they and other sea-birds kept up around us, that we knew not which way to look —for they covered the rocks in thousands; but, as we continued to gaze, we observed several four-legged animals (as we thought) walking in the middle of the penguins.

" Pull in a bit," cried Peterkin, " and let's see what these are. They must be fond of noisy company, to live with such creatures."

To our surprise we found that these were no other than penguins which had gone down on all-fours, and were walking among the bushes on their feet and wings. Suddenly one big old bird, that had been sitting on a point very near to us, gazing in silent surprise, became alarmed, and running down the rocks, fell, rather than ran, into the sea. It dived in a moment, and, a few seconds afterwards, came out of the water far ahead, with such a jump, and such a dive back into the sea again, that we could scarcely believe it was not a fish that had leaped in sport.

" That beats everything," said Peterkin, rubbing his nose, and putting on an expression of surprise and anger. " I've heard of a thing being neither fish, flesh, nor bird, but I never did expect to live to see an animal that was all three together—at once—in one! But look there! " he continued, pointing with a tired look to the shore. " Look there! there's no end to it. What *has* that bird got under its tail? "

We turned to look in the direction pointed out, and there saw a penguin walking slowly along the shore with an egg under its tail. There were several others, we observed, doing the same thing; and we found afterwards that these were a kind of penguins that always carried their eggs so. Indeed, they had a most useful pocket for the purpose, just between the tail and the legs. We were very much struck with the regularity and order of this colony. The island seemed to be divided up into squares, of which each penguin possessed one, and sat in stiff graveness in the middle of it, or took a slow march up and down the spaces between. Some were sitting on their eggs, but others were feeding their young ones in a manner that caused us to laugh not a little. The mother stood on a raised rock, while the young one stood patiently below her on the ground. Suddenly the mother raised her head and uttered a number of loud, unpleasant noises.

" She's going to be ill," cried Peterkin.

But this was not the case, although she looked like it. In a few seconds she put down her head and opened her mouth, into which the young one put its beak and seemed to take something from her throat. Then the noise was repeated, the eating continued, and so the operation of feeding was carried on till the young one was satisfied; but what she fed her little one with we could not tell.

" Now, just look over there! " said Peterkin, in an interested tone. " If that isn't the worst piece of motherly conduct I ever saw! That wicked old lady penguin has just thrown her young one into the sea, and there's another about to follow her example."

This indeed seemed to be the case, for on the top of a steep rock close to the edge of the sea we observed an old penguin trying to get her young one into the water; but the young one seemed very unwilling to go, and moved very slowly towards her. At last she went gently behind the young bird and pushed it a little towards the water, but with great tenderness, as much as to say, " Don't be afraid, dear; I won't hurt you, my little one! " but no sooner did she get it to the edge of the rock, where it stood looking thoughtfully down at the sea, than she gave it a sudden, hard push, sending it head first down the slope into the water, where its mother left it to swim to the shore as it best could. We observed many of them doing this, and we thus learnt that this is the way in which old penguins teach their children to swim.

Scarcely had we finished making our observations on this, when we were surprised by about a dozen of the old birds jumping in the most unsafe and funny manner towards the sea. The beach here was a sloping rock, and when they came to it some of them jumped down in safety, but others lost their balance, and rolled and fell down the slope in the most helpless manner. The instant they reached the water, however, they seemed to be in their proper place. They dived and bounded out of it and into it again with the greatest ease; and so, diving and bounding —for they could not fly—they went rapidly out to sea.

On seeing this, Peterkin turned with a grave face to us and said, " It's my opinion that these birds are all completely and entirely mad, and that this is a magic island. I therefore say that we should either put about ship and fly in terror from the spot, or land bravely on the island, and fight as hard as we can."

" I vote for landing; so pull in, lads," said Jack, giving a stroke with his oar that made the boat turn.

In a few seconds we ran the boat into a little bay, where we made her fast to a piece of coral, and running up the beach, entered the ranks of the penguins armed with our sticks and our spear. We were greatly surprised to find that, instead of attacking us or showing signs of fear at our approach, these strange birds did not move from their places until we took hold of them, and merely turned their eyes on us in wonder as we passed.

There was one old penguin, however, that began to walk slowly towards the sea, and Peterkin took it into his head that he would try to stop it, so he ran between it and the sea and waved his stick in its face. But this proved to be a determined old bird. It would not go back; in fact, it would not cease to advance, but battled with Peterkin bravely, and drove him before it until it reached the sea. Had Peterkin used his stick he could easily have killed it, no doubt; but as he had no wish to do so cruel an act merely out of sport, he let the bird escape.

We spent fully three hours on this island in watching these strange birds, and when we finally left them, we all three decided, after much talking, that they were the most wonderful creatures we had ever seen; and further, we thought it probable that they were the most wonderful creatures in the world!

CHAPTER 16

ANOTHER STORM

IT was evening before we left the island of the penguins. As we had made up our minds to camp for the night on a small island, on which grew a few coconut trees, about two miles off, we used our oars with some energy. But a danger was in store for us which we had not expected. The wind, which had carried us so quickly to Penguin Island, increased as evening drew on, and before we had gone half the distance to the small island, it became a bad storm. Although it was not so directly against us as to prevent our rowing in the course we wished to go, yet it checked us very much. And although the force of the sea was somewhat broken by the island, the waves soon began to rise, and to roll their broken heads against our small boat, so that she began to take in water, and we had much difficulty in keeping our boat from going down. At last the wind and sea together became so terrible that we found it impossible to reach the island, so Jack suddenly put the head of the boat round and ordered Peterkin and me to set a corner of the sail, intending to run back to Penguin Island.

" We shall at least have the shelter of the bushes," he said, as the boat flew before the wind, " and the penguins will keep us company."

As Jack spoke, the wind suddenly changed and began to blow so much against us that we were forced to put up more of the sail in order to reach the island, being by this change thrown much to the side of it. What made matters worse was, that the storm came in bursts, so that we were more than once nearly upset.

" Stand by, both of you," cried Jack, in a quick, earnest tone; " be ready to let down the sail. I very much fear we won't make the island after all."

Peterkin and I were so much used to trusting everything to Jack that we had fallen into the way of not considering things, especially such things as were under Jack's care. We had, therefore, never doubted for a moment that all was going well, so that it was with no little fear that we heard him make the above statement. However, we had no time for question, for at the moment he spoke a heavy burst of wind was coming towards us, and as we were then flying with one side going occasionally under the waves, it was clear that we should have to lower our sail altogether.

In a few seconds the storm struck the boat, but Peterkin and I had the sail down in a moment, so that it did not turn us over; but when it was past we were more than half full of water. This I soon threw out, while Peterkin again put up a corner of the sail; but the evil which Jack had feared came upon us. We found it quite impossible to make Penguin Island. The storm carried us quickly past it towards the open sea, and the terrible truth came to us that we should be carried out and left to die slowly in a small boat in the middle of the wide ocean.

This idea was forced very strongly upon us, because we saw nothing in the direction in which the wind was blowing us save the fierce waves of the sea; and, indeed, we were afraid as we gazed round us, for we were now beyond the shelter of the islands, and it seemed as though any of the huge waves, which curled over in masses of angry water might swallow us up in a moment. The water, also, began to wash in over our sides, and I had to keep constantly throwing it out, for Jack had to guide the boat, and Peterkin could not quit the sail for an instant without putting our lives in danger. Suddenly Jack uttered a cry of hope, and pointed towards a low island or rock which lay directly in front. We had not seen it before, owing to the dark clouds in the sky and the blinding drops of water that seemed to fill the whole air.

As we neared this rock we observed that there were no trees or other plants on it, and that it was so low that the sea broke completely over it. In fact, it was nothing more than the top of one of the coral rocks, which rose only a few feet above the level of the water, and, in stormy weather, could only just be seen. Over this island the waves were breaking with great force, and our hearts were filled with fear as we saw that there was not a spot where we could put our little boat without its being dashed to pieces.

" Show a little bit more sail," cried Jack, as we were sweeping past the weather side of the rock with fearful speed.

Peterkin put up about a foot more of our sail. Little though the addition was, it caused the boat to lie over so much, as we rushed through the angry waves, that I expected it to turn over every instant; and I blamed Jack in my heart for his boldness. But I did him injustice, for although during two seconds the water rushed into the boat in a river, he succeeded in guiding us sharply round to the sheltered side of the rock, where the water was calmer and the force of the wind broken.

" Out your oars now, boys! That's well done. Row!"

THE CAVE

We obeyed instantly. The oars went into the waves together. One good hard pull, and we were floating in a calm opening that was so narrow as to be just able to admit our boat. Here we were in perfect safety, and as we leaped on shore and fastened our rope to the rocks, I thanked God in my heart for our deliverance from so great danger.

But although I have said we were now in safety, I think that few of my readers would have liked to be in our place. It is true we had no lack of food, but we were wet to the skin; the sea was beating round us and the water flying over our heads, so that we were completely clothed, as it were, in water. The spot on which we had landed was not more than twelve yards across, and from this spot we could not move without the chance of being carried away by the storm. At the upper end of the bay was a small hollow or cave in the rock, which sheltered us from the force of the winds and waves; and as the rock extended over our heads, it prevented the drops of water from falling upon us.

" Why," said Peterkin, beginning to feel cheerful again, " it seems to me that we have got into a fish's cave, for there is nothing but water all round us; and as for earth or sky, they are things of the past."

Peterkin's idea was more than a fancy, for what with the sea roaring in white waves up to our very feet, and the water flying in white sheets continually over our heads, and more water dropping heavily from the rock above like a curtain in front of our cave, it did seem to us very much more like being below than above water.

" Now, boys," cried Jack, " let's make ourselves comfortable. Toss out our food, Peterkin; and here, Ralph, help me to pull up the boat. Make haste."

We were much cheered by the cheerful manner of our companion. Fortunately the cave, although not very deep, was quite dry, so that we succeeded in making ourselves much more comfortable than could have been expected. We landed our food, dried our garments, spread our sail below us, and after having eaten a good meal, began to feel quite cheerful. But as night drew on our spirits went down again, for with the daylight all proof of our security disappeared. We could no longer see the firm rock on which we lay, while the storm roared loudly round us.

The night grew perfectly dark as it advanced, so that we could not see our hands when we held them up before our eyes, and were obliged to feel each other occasionally to make sure that we were safe, for the storm at last became so terrible that it was difficult to make our voices heard. A slight change of the wind, as we supposed, caused a few drops of water ever and again to blow into our faces; and the sea, in its mad boiling, washed up into our little bay until it reached our feet and threatened to tear away our boat. In order to prevent this latter misfortune, we pulled the boat farther up and held the rope in our hands.

Occasional flashes of lightning showed us the fearful scene all round us. Yet we longed for those flashes, for they were less terrible than the thick blackness that succeeded them. The thunder seemed to tear the skies in two, and fell upon our ears through the wild shouting of the storm as if it had been but a gentle summer wind; while the waves burst upon the weather side of the island until we fancied that the rock was giving way, and in our terror we held on to the bare ground, expecting every moment to be carried away into the black sea. Oh, it was a night of terrible fear! and no one can imagine the feelings of joy with which we at last saw the dawn of day break through the clouds round us.

For three days and three nights we remained on this rock, while the storm continued. On the morning of the fourth day it suddenly ceased, and the wind fell completely; but the waves still ran so high that we did not dare to put off in our boat. During the greater part of this period we had scarcely gone to sleep for more than a few minutes at a time, but on the third night we were soon asleep. Early on the fourth morning we found the sea very much down, and the sun shining brightly again in the clear blue sky.

WE RETURN

It was with light hearts that we set forth once more in our little boat, and rowed away for our island home, which, we were happy to find, was in sight in the distance, for we had feared that we had been blown entirely out of sight of it. As it was perfectly calm, we had to row during the greater part of the day; but towards the afternoon a fair wind came on, which allowed us to put up our sail. We soon passed Penguin Island, and the other island which we had failed to reach on the day the storm commenced. But as we had still enough food, and were anxious to get home, we did not land, to the great sorrow of Peterkin, who seemed to be very fond of the penguins.

Although the wind was pretty fresh for several hours, we did not reach the outer reef of our island till nightfall, and before we had sailed more than a hundred yards into the lagoon, the wind died away altogether, so that we had to take to our oars again. It was late, and the moon and stars were shining brightly when we arrived opposite the house and leaped upon the shore. So glad were we to be safe back again on our island, that we scarcely took time to drag the boat a short way up the beach, and then ran up to see that all was right at the house. I must say, however, that my joy was mixed with a sort of fear in case our home had been visited and destroyed while we were away; but on reaching it we found everything just as it had been left.

CHAPTER 17

A BATTLE

FOR many months after this we continued to live on our island in great peace and happiness. Sometimes we went out fishing in the lagoon, and sometimes went hunting in the woods, or climbed to the mountain-top, by way of a change, although Peterkin always said that we went for the purpose of calling to any ship that might chance to come in sight. But I am certain that none of us wished to be taken out of our prison, for we were extremely happy, and Peterkin used to say that as we were very young we should not feel the loss of a year or two. Peterkin, as I have said before, was fourteen years of age, Jack eighteen, and I fifteen. But Jack was very tall, strong, and manly for his age, and might easily have been mistaken for twenty.

OUR EMPLOYMENTS

The weather was beautiful, and as many of the fruit-trees continued to bear fruit and blossom all the year round, we never wanted for a plentiful supply of food. The pigs, too, seemed rather to increase than become fewer, although Peterkin was very frequent in his attacks on them with his spear. If at any time we failed in finding a herd, we had only to pay a visit to the tree under which we first saw them, where we always found a large family of them asleep under its branches.

We employed ourselves very busily during this time in making various garments of coconut cloth, as those with which we had landed were beginning to be very worn. Peterkin also made excellent shoes out of the skin of the old pig, in the following manner:—He first cut a piece of the hide a few inches longer than his foot. This he left for some time in water, and while it was wet he sewed up one end of it, so as to form a rough back to a shoe. This done, he bored a row of holes all round the edge of the piece of skin, through which a line was passed. Into the sewed-up part of this shoe he pushed his heel, then drawing the string tight, the edges rose up and came over his foot all round. It is true there were a great many ill-looking places in these shoes, but we found them very serviceable, all the same, and Jack came at last to prefer them to his long boots.

We also made various other useful articles, which added to our comfort, and once or twice spoke of building us a big house. But we liked our present one so much, and found it so serviceable that we determined not to leave it, nor to attempt the building of another house, which in such a country might turn out to be rather unpleasant than useful.

Diving in the Water Garden also still gave us as much pleasure as ever; and Peterkin began to be a little more used to the water from constant practice. As for Jack and me, we began to feel as if water were our native place, and spent so much time in it that Peterkin said he feared we would turn into fish some day, and swim off and leave him; adding that he had been for a long time observing that Jack was becoming more and more like a shark every day. Whereupon Jack replied that if he, Peterkin, were changed into a fish, he would certainly turn into nothing better or bigger than a crab.

Poor Peterkin was not so sad at being unable to come with us in our delightful dives under water, except, indeed, when Jack would dive down to the bottom of the Water Garden, sit down on a rock and look up and make faces at him. Peterkin did then often say he would give anything to be able to do that. I laughed when Peterkin said this; for if he could only have seen his own face when he happened to take a short dive, he would have seen that Jack's was easily beaten by it: the great difference being, however, that Jack made faces on purpose—Peterkin couldn't help it!

Now, while we were engaged with these occupations, an event occurred one day which was as unexpected as it was alarming and horrible.

CANOES APPEAR

Jack and I were sitting, as we often used to do, on the rocks above Diamond Cave. Peterkin was getting the water from his garments, having just fallen into the sea—a thing he was constantly doing—when our attention was suddenly drawn to two objects which appeared on the sky-line.

" What are they; do you know? " I said, addressing Jack.

" I can't think," answered he. " I've noticed them for some time, and fancied they were black sea-birds, but the more I look at them the more I feel convinced they are much larger than birds."

" They seem to be coming towards us," said I.

" Hallo! What's wrong? " asked Peterkin, coming up.

" Look there," said Jack.

" Fish! " cried Peterkin, shading his eyes with his hand. " No—eh—*can* they be boats, Jack? "

Our hearts beat with joy at the very thought of seeing human faces again.

" I think you are about right, Peterkin. But they seem to me to move strangely for boats," said Jack, in a low tone, as if he were talking to himself.

I noticed that a shade of alarm crossed Jack's face as he gazed long at the two objects, which were now nearing us fast. At last he jumped to his feet.

"They are canoes, Ralph! Whether war-canoes or not I cannot tell; but this I know, that all the natives of the South Sea Islands are fierce man-eaters, and they have little respect for strangers. We must hide if they land here, which I earnestly hope they will not do."

WE HIDE

I was greatly alarmed at Jack's speech, but I thought less of what he said than of the earnest, anxious manner in which he said it, and it was with very uncomfortable feelings that Peterkin and I followed him quickly into the woods.

" What a pity," said I, as we gained the shelter of the bushes, " that we have forgotten our arms!"

" It doesn't matter," said Jack. " Here are sticks enough and to spare."

As he spoke he laid his hand on a number of thick poles of various sizes, which Peterkin's ever-busy hands had formed during our frequent visits to the place, for no other purpose, it would seem, than that of having something to do.

We each selected a thick stick according to our several tastes, and lay down behind a rock, whence we could see the canoes approach, without ourselves being seen. At first we said a word or two now and then on their appearance, but after they entered the lagoon, and drew near the beach, we ceased to speak, and gazed with the greatest interest at the scene before us.

We now observed that the first canoe was being chased by the other, and that it contained a few women and children, as well as men—perhaps forty souls in all; while the boat which pursued it contained only men. They seemed to be about the same in number, but were better armed, and had the appearance of being a war-party. Both crews were paddling with all their might, and it seemed as if the men behind paddled hard themselves to catch the others before they could land. In this, however, they failed.

The first canoe made for the beach close beneath the rocks

behind which we were hidden. Their short oars flashed in the water, and sent up a constant shower of drops. The water curled from the front, and the eyes of the rowers were shining in their black faces as they rowed with all their force; nor did they stop till the canoe struck the beach with a shock. Then with a shout the whole party jumped, as if by magic, from the canoe to the shore. Three women, two of whom carried babies in their arms, rushed into the woods; and the men crowded to the water's edge, with stones in their hands, spears and sticks raised, to prevent their enemies from coming on shore.

The distance between the two canoes had been about half a mile, and, at the great speed they were going, this was soon passed. As the second boat neared the shore, no sign of fear could be noticed. On they came like a wild horse—received but took no notice of a shower of stones. The canoe struck, and with a shout they leaped into the water, and drove their enemies up the beach.

THE BATTLE

The battle that immediately took place was frightful to behold. Most of the men used sticks of huge size and strange shapes, with which they beat in each other's heads. As they wore almost no clothes, and had to bound, leap, and run in their terrible hand-to-hand fights, they looked more like devils than human beings. I felt my heart grow sick at the sight of this bloody battle, and would have liked to have turned away, but something seemed to hold me down and keep my eyes upon the fighting men. I observed that the attacking party was led by a most strange being, who, from his size and strangeness, I thought was a chief. His hair stood out, so that it looked like a large hat. It was a light yellow colour, which surprised me much, for the man's body was as black as coal, and I felt certain that the hair must have been coloured. He was painted from

"The men crowded to the water's edge with spears and sticks."

head to foot. With his yellow hair, his huge black frame, his shining eyes and white teeth, he seemed the most terrible monster I ever saw. He was very terrible in the fight, and had already killed four men.

Suddenly the yellow-haired chief was attacked by a man quite as strong and large as himself. He waved a heavy club something like an eagle's beak at the point. For a second or two these huge men watched one another, moving round and round as if to gain an advantage; but seeing that nothing was to be gained by this, and that the loss of time might turn the tide of battle either way, they made up their minds to attack at the same instant, for, with a wild shout and jump, I saw them swing their heavy sticks, which met with a loud report. Suddenly the yellow-haired native tripped, his enemy jumped forward, the great stick went up, but it did not come down, for at that moment the man was knocked down by a stone from the hand of one who had witnessed his chief's danger.

This was the end of the battle. The natives who landed first turned and ran towards the bush, on seeing the fall of their chief. But not one escaped. They were all caught and knocked over. I saw, however, that they were not all killed. Indeed, their enemies, now that they were conquered, seemed anxious to take them alive; and they succeeded in securing fifteen, whom they bound hand and foot with ropes, and carrying them up into the woods, laid them down among the bushes. Here they left them, for what purpose I knew not, and came back to the scene of the late battle, where the rest of the party were washing their wounds.

Out of the forty blacks that made up the attacking party, only twenty-eight remained alive, two of whom were sent into the bush to hunt for the women and children. Of the other party, as I have said, only fifteen were left, and these were lying bound and helpless on the grass.

Jack and Peterkin and I now looked at each other, and whispered our fears that the natives might climb up the rocks to search for fresh water, and so discover the place where we were hiding; but we were so much interested in watching their movements that we agreed to remain where we were—and, indeed, we could not easily have risen without showing ourselves. One of the natives now went up to the wood, and soon came with wood, and we were not a little surprised to see him set fire to it in the very same way as Jack had done the time we made our first fire—with the bow and drill.

When the fire was burning, two of the party went again to the woods and came back with one of the bound men. A terrible feeling began to creep over my heart as the thought flashed upon me that they were going to burn their enemies. As they bore him to the fire my feelings were almost too much for me. I breathed deeply, and seizing my stick, tried to jump to my feet; but Jack's powerful arm held me to the earth. Next moment one of the natives raised his club, and beat in the unhappy creature's head. He must have died instantly; and strange though it may seem, I had a feeling of pleasure when the deed was done, because I now knew that the poor man could not be burned alive. Scarcely had his limbs ceased to move when the natives cut pieces of flesh from his body, and, after roasting them slightly over the fire, ate them.

PRISONERS

Suddenly there came a cry from the woods, and in a few seconds the two natives hastened towards the fire dragging the three women and their two babies along with them. One of those women was much younger than her companions, and we were struck with the gentle look on her face, which, although she had the flat nose and thick lips of the others, was of a light brown colour, and we thought that she must be of a different race. She and her companions wore short skirts. Their hair was perfectly black, but instead of being long, was short and curly—though not woolly—somewhat like the hair of a young boy.

While we gazed with interest and some anxiety at these poor creatures, the big chief advanced to one of the elder women and laid his hand upon the child. But the mother drew back from him, and holding the little one to her bosom, uttered a cry of fear. With a cruel laugh, the chief tore the child from her arms and tossed it into the sea. A low sound burst from Jack's lips as he witnessed this wicked act and heard the mother's cry, as she fell fainting on the sand. The little waves rolled the child on the beach, as if they refused to be a party in such a wicked act, and we could observe that the little one still lived.

The young girl was now brought forward, and the chief addressed her; but although we heard his voice and even the words clearly, of course we could not understand what he said. The girl made no answer to his fierce questions, and we saw by the way in which he pointed to the fire that he threatened her life.

" Peterkin," said Jack, in a whisper, " have you got your knife? "

" Yes," replied Peterkin, whose face was pale as death.

" That will do. Listen to me, and obey my orders quickly. Here is the small knife, Ralph. Fly, both of you, through the bush, cut the ropes that bind the prisoners, and set them free. There, quick, before it is too late." Jack jumped up, and seized a heavy but short stick, while his strong frame trembled with anger, and large drops rolled down his face.

TO THE RESCUE

At this moment the man who had killed the native a few minutes before advanced towards the girl with his heavy stick. Jack uttered a shout that rang like a death-cry among the rocks. With one bound he leaped over a side of the rock full fifteen feet high, and before the natives had recovered from their surprise, was in the middle of them; while Peterkin and I dashed through the bushes towards the prisoners. With one blow of his stick Jack felled the man with the club, then turning round with a look of terrible anger, he rushed upon the big chief with the yellow hair. If the blow which Jack aimed at his head had taken effect, the huge native would have needed no second stroke; but he was quick as a cat, and avoided it by jumping to one side, at the same time swinging his heavy stick at the head of his foe.

It was now Jack's turn to leap away, and well was it for him that the first burst of his blind anger was over, else he had been an easy foe for his huge enemy; but Jack was cool now. He made his blows rapidly and well, and the great value of his light stick was proved in this fight; for while he could easily avoid the blows of the chief's heavy stick, the chief could not so easily avoid those of his light one. But he was so quick, and his stick was so frightful, that although Jack struck him almost every blow, the strokes had to be delivered so quickly that they wanted force.

It was a good thing for Jack that the other natives considered the success of their chief in this fight to be so certain that they did not come to his help. Had they doubted it, they would have probably ended the matter at once by felling him. But they contented themselves with waiting to see what happened.

The force which the chief had to spend in using his stick now began to be clear. He moved more slowly, he breathed hard, and the surprised natives drew nearer in order to assist him. Jack observed this. He felt that his fate was certain, and decided to cast his life upon the next blow. The chief's club was again about to descend on his head. He might have avoided it easily, but instead of doing so, he suddenly shortened his hold of his own club, rushed in under the blow, struck his enemy right between the eyes with all his force, and fell to the earth, crushed beneath the body of the chief.

A dozen clubs flew high in air, ready to descend on the head of Jack; but they waited a moment, for the huge body of the chief completely covered him. That moment saved his life. Before the natives could tear the chief's body away, seven of their number fell beneath the clubs of the prisoners whom Peterkin and I had set free, and two others fell under our own hands. We could never have done this had not our enemies been so taken up with the fight between Jack and their chief that they had failed to observe us until we were upon them. They still had three more men than we had; but we were joyful with victory, while they were taken by surprise and shocked by the fall of their chief. Besides, they were surprised by the sweeping anger of Jack, who seemed to have lost his senses completely, and had no sooner shaken himself free of the chief's body than he rushed into the middle of them, and with three blows our numbers were equal. Peterkin and I flew to help him, the natives followed us, and in less than ten minutes the whole of our enemies were knocked down or made prisoners, bound hand and foot, and stretched out side by side upon the seashore.

CHAPTER 18

ALONE AGAIN

AFTER the battle was over, the natives crowded round us and gazed at us in surprise, while they continued to pour upon us a flood of questions, which of course we could not answer. However, by way of putting an end to it, Jack took the chief (who had recovered from the effects of his wound) by the hand and shook it warmly. No sooner did the blacks see that this was meant to express our good wishes than they shook hands with us all round. After this was gone through Jack went up to the girl, who had never once moved from the rock where she had been left, but had continued eagerly watching all that had passed. He made signs to her to follow him, and then, taking the chief by the hand, was about to conduct him to the house, when his eye fell on the poor baby which had been thrown into the sea and was still lying on the shore. Dropping the chief's hand he hastened towards it, and to his great joy found it to be still alive. We also found that the mother was beginning to recover slowly.

" Here. get out of the way," said Jack, pushing us on one side, as we bent over the poor woman and tried to restore her. " I'll soon bring her round."

So saying, he placed the baby on her bosom, and laid its warm cheek on hers. The effect was wonderful. The woman opened her eyes, felt the child, looked at it, and with a cry of joy took it in her arms, at the same time trying to rise, for the purpose, it would seem, of rushing into the woods.

" There, that's all right," said Jack, once more taking the chief by the hand. " Now, Ralph and Peterkin, make the women and these fellows follow me to the house. We'll feed them as well as we can."

In a few minutes the natives were all seated on the ground in front of the house making a good meal off a cold roast pig, several ducks, and cold fish, together with a large supply of coconuts, bread-fruits, yams, taro, and fruit; with all of which they seemed to be quite familiar and perfectly satisfied.

While they were eating, we three, being thoroughly tired with our day's work, took a good drink from a coconut, and throwing ourselves in our beds, fell fast asleep. The natives, it seems, did so too, and in half an hour the whole camp was sleeping.

How long we slept I cannot tell, but this I know, that when we lay down the sun was setting, and when we awoke it was high in the heavens. I awakened Jack, who jumped up in surprise, and could not at first understand our situation.

" Now, then," said he, " let's see after breakfast. Hallo, Peterkin, lazy fellow! How long do you mean to lie there? "

Peterkin rubbed his eyes. " Well," said he, looking up after some trouble, " if it isn't to-morrow morning, and me thinking it was to-day all this time! Hallo, beauty! Where did you come from? You seem quite at home, anyhow. Bah! might as well speak to a cat as to you."

This was called forth by the sight of one of the elderly women, who had seated herself on the rock in front of the house, and, having placed her child at her feet, was busily engaged in eating the remains of a roast pig.

By this time the natives outside were all up, and breakfast nearly ready. During the course of it we several times tried to speak with the natives by signs, but without effect. At last we hit upon a plan of discovering their names. Jack pointed to his chest and said " Jack " very clearly; then he pointed to Peterkin and to me, repeating our names at the same time. Then he pointed to himself again, and said " Jack," and laying his finger on the chest of the chief, looked clearly into his face. The chief instantly understood him, and said " Tararo " twice clearly. Jack repeated it after him, and the chief, nodding his head, said " Chuck." On hearing which Peterkin burst out laughing; but Jack turned, and said, " I must look even more angry than I feel, Peterkin, for these fellows don't like to be laughed at." Then turning towards the youngest of the women, who was seated at the door of the house, he pointed to her; at which the chief said " Avatea."

Jack now made signs to the natives to follow him, and taking up his axe, he led them to the place where the battle had been fought. Here we found the prisoners, who had passed the night on the beach, having been completely forgotten by us, as our minds had been full of our guests, until we went to sleep. They did not seem the worse for their night on the beach, however, as we judged by the way in which they ate the breakfast that was soon after given to them.

Jack then began to make a hole in the sand, and after working a few seconds, he pointed to it, and to the dead bodies that lay on the beach. The natives immediately saw what he wanted, and running for their paddles, made a hole in the course of half an

"We gave him a piece of wood with our names cut on it."

hour that was quite large enough to contain all the bodies of the dead. When it was finished they tossed their dead enemies into it with so little feeling that we felt certain they would not have put themselves to this trouble if we had not asked them to do so. The body of the yellow-haired chief was the last thrown in. This poor man would have recovered from the blow with which Jack knocked him down, and indeed he did try to rise during the fight that followed his fall; but one of his enemies, happening to notice the action, gave him a blow with his stick that killed him on the spot.

THE NATIVES DEPART

When the boat was ready, we assisted the natives to carry the prisoners into it, and helped them to load it with food. Peterkin also went into the woods for the purpose of making a special attack upon the pigs, and killed no less than six of them. These we baked and presented to our friends on the day that they went away. On that day Tararo made a great many signs to us, which, after much talking, we came to understand were to ask us to go away with him to his island; but having no desire to do so, we shook our heads very decidedly. We gave him a piece of wood with our names cut on it, and a piece of string to hang it round his neck.

In a few minutes more we were all on the beach. Being unable to speak to the natives, we shook hands with them, and expected they would depart; but before doing so, Tararo went up to Jack and rubbed noses with him, after which he did the same with Peterkin and me! Seeing that this was their way of saying farewell, we determined to use their custom, so we rubbed noses with the whole party, women and all! Avatea was the last to take leave of us, and we felt a feeling of real sorrow when she approached to bid us farewell. Besides her gentle manners, she was the only one of the party who showed the smallest sign of sadness at parting from us. Going up to Jack, she put out her flat little nose to be rubbed, and after that did the same to Peterkin and me.

An hour later the canoe was out of sight, and we, with a feeling of sadness creeping round our hearts, were seated in silence beneath the shadow of our house, thinking of the wonderful doings of the last few days.

CHAPTER 19

GOOD-BYE TO THE CORAL ISLAND

ONE day we were all enjoying ourselves in the Water Garden before going fishing; for Peterkin had kept us in such constant supply of pigs that we had become quite tired of them, and desired a change. Peterkin was sitting on the rock, while we were creeping among the rocks under the water. Happening to look up, I observed Peterkin making signs for us to come up, so I gave Jack a push and rose immediately.

"A sail! A sail! Ralph, look! Jack, away on the sky-line there, just over the entrance to the lagoon!" cried Peterkin, as we climbed up the rocks.

"So it is, a ship!" said Jack, as he began to dress in haste.

Our hearts were thrown into a terrible state by this discovery, for if it should touch at our island we had no doubt the captain would be happy to take us to some of the other islands, where we could find a ship sailing for England or some other part of Europe. Home, with all that it meant, rushed in upon my heart like a flood, and much though I loved the Coral Island and the house which had now been our home so long, I felt that I could have quitted all at that moment without a sigh. With hope and joy we hastened to the highest point of rock near our house, and waited for the vessel, for we now saw that she was making straight for the island, under a strong wind.

In less than an hour she was close to the reef, where she rounded to, and stopped in order to look at the coast. Seeing this, and fearing that they might not see us, we all three waved pieces of coconut cloth in the air, and soon saw them beginning to get a boat into the water and run busily about the decks as if they meant to land.

OUR FAREWELL VISITS

Next day we paid a farewell visit to the different familiar spots where most of our time had been spent. We climbed the mountain-top, and gazed for the last time at the rich green trees in the valleys, the white sandy beach, the calm lagoon, and the coral reef with its great waves. Then we descended to the rocks above Diamond Cave, and looked down at the pale green animal which we had made such vain efforts to spear in days gone by. From this we hurried to the Water Garden, and took a last dive into its clear waters, and played for the last time among its corals. I hurried out before my companions, and dressed in haste, in order to have a long look at my hole in the rock. It was in fine condition—the water perfectly clear; the red and green seaweed of the brightest colours; the red, purple, yellow and green flower-animals with their arms fully spread out, and stretched as if to welcome their former master; and the shellfish, as Peterkin said, looking as fine as ever. It was indeed so lovely and so interesting that I would scarcely allow myself to be torn away from it.

Last of all, we came back to the house and collected the few articles we possessed. These we took on board in our little boat, after having cut our names on a piece of iron-wood, thus:

JACK MARTIN
RALPH ROVER
PETERKIN GAY

which we fixed up inside the house. The boat was then taken on board and the ship moved off. A strong wind was blowing off shore when we set sail, at a little before sunset. It swept us quickly past the reef and out to sea. The shore quickly grew more faint as the shades of evening fell, while our ship bounded lightly over the waves. Slowly the mountain-top went down on the sky-line, until it became a mere spot. In another moment the sun and the Coral Island faded away together into the broad bosom of the Pacific.

QUESTIONS

(Ralph Rover tells the story. Although he is not named in the first chapter, the name Ralph is used in the questions.)

CHAPTER 1

1 What did Ralph do between the age of twelve and the age of fifteen?
2 Who first told him about the Coral Islands?
3 What did he say to make his father let him go to the South Seas?
4 Who were Ralph's special friends on the *Arrow*?
5 What did the three friends think when they passed coral islands?
6 How long did the great storm last?
7 What was Jack's plan for saving his friends and himself?
8 What happened to the ship's boat?

CHAPTER 2

1 How long was it before Ralph recovered his senses?
2 What had made him lose his senses?
3 How did Jack find out what happened to the ship?
4 Why was Ralph unhappy when he heard what had happened?
5 What did Jack wish they had?
6 What two things did Jack say they must do?

CHAPTER 3

1 Whose knife had they?
2 Who brought the telescope to the island, and how?
3 How did Jack show kindness to Ralph?
4 Why were the waves which broke on the beach only small ones?
5 How did the axe come to the island?
6 What did the three friends drink?
7 How had Jack learnt about coconuts?
8 What two ways of making a fire are mentioned in this chapter?

CHAPTER 4

1 What made Peterkin wake up?
2 Why did the boys not know what the time was?
3 What made Jack wake up?
4 Which of the boys was the best swimmer?
5 What made Jack swallow water?
6 What did the boys eat for breakfast?

CHAPTER 5

1 What weapon did each of the boys carry on the journey?
2 Why did Jack not carry his stick?
3 Make a list of the things Jack told the others about the bread-fruit tree.
4 How did Jack know about the bread-fruit tree?
5 Why did Jack push Peterkin into the bushes?
6 Why did they not pick bread-fruit at once?
7 Why did the boys climb the second mountain?
8 Why were there always waves breaking on the reef?

CHAPTER 6

1 Why did the boys not make their home in the cave?
2 How did Jack make a knife?
3 Why did they want to have a log in the water?
4 They all fell into the water when Peterkin caught his first fish. Why?
5 How did Jack know the shark would attack them?
6 What did he do to stop the shark from biting?

CHAPTER 7

1 What used Jack to do to make Ralph laugh under water?
2 What were they looking for when they found the Water Garden?
3 How did Ralph learn more about the sea creatures?
4 Why did they plan to travel round the island?
5 Why did they decide to make one bow instead of three?
6 How did Jack make a light?
7 What weapons did Peterkin and Ralph make for themselves?
8 What happened while they were working?
9 What did each boy find out when he began to practise with his weapon?
10 Why did Ralph and Peterkin owe much of their success to Jack?

CHAPTER 8

1 What two things did Ralph take on the journey besides his sling?
2 Why did Ralph think that Peterkin's stick was "not worth a button"?
3 What did the boys think was the cause of the clouds of water?
4 How did they dry their clothes?
5 How did they try to reach the strange fish-like object?
6 What did Ralph decide to do about the object?

CHAPTER 9

1 Explain what Peterkin meant when he said that Jack was "talking bad English" about the banyan tree.
2 What other curious tree did they find?
3 Why did they try to kill one of the brightly coloured birds?
4 Who killed one, and how?
5 How did Peterkin get Jack's arrow back?
6 How did they cook: (a) the pig, (b) the yam and taro, (c) the bird?

CHAPTER 10

1 What made the dreadful cry?
2 Why did the penguins look like soldiers?
3 What was noticeable about coconut palms?
4 How long did it take the boys to walk round the island?
5 How do you know they were tired after their journey?
6 Why were they afraid of losing count of a day?
7 What did Ralph think was the strangest animal in his rock pool?
8 What do *you* think was the most interesting thing in the rock pool?

CHAPTER 11

1 Why was Jack the first to dive down to the strange green object?
2 Why were the other two boys frightened?
3 How long did Jack remain under water after his dive?
4 What used Jack always to do when he came up after a dive?
5 How did Jack explain the green object?
6 How did Jack and Ralph make a light with which to explore the cave?

CHAPTER 12

1 How did Jack drive the pigs towards the other boys?
2 What happened to Peterkin when the pigs first came over the hill?
3 Why did Ralph not try to kill a second pig?
4 Why were Jack and Ralph surprised when Peterkin killed the old pig?
5 What was Peterkin's reason for killing the old pig?
6 How did they carry the old pig home?

CHAPTER 13

1 What did Jack use to make the frame of the boat?
2 What did he use for boards?
3 How did the boys make rope?
4 How were the boards fastened together?
5 What was the boys' table?
6 What might there be on the table for a "feast"?
7 How did Jack hope to make a sail?
8 How long did it take Jack and Ralph to make oars?

CHAPTER 14

1 When the boat was ready, where did they go first?
2 What did the boys notice as they dragged the boat up the beach?
3 How long did it take the boys to make a mast and sail?
4 How was the sail made?
5 What did Jack do to stop the bottom of the boat from wearing off?
6 What hooks did Peterkin use, and which was the best hook?

Questions

CHAPTER 15

1. Why did they take food with them when they went to Penguin Island?
2. Why was Peterkin so good at killing pigs?
3. What difficulty did they find in getting the boat out past the reef?
4. Why did they not go round the island inside the reef?
5. How near to Penguin Island did the wind take them?
6. For what purpose did the penguins use their wings?
7. How did the penguins on Penguin Island carry their eggs?
8. How did the penguins feed their young ones?
9. How were the young penguins taught to swim?
10. How long did the boys spend on Penguin Island?

CHAPTER 16

1. What work did each of the boys do during the storm?
2. Where did they find shelter from the storm?
3. Why were they more afraid when it became dark?
4. How long did the storm last?
5. Why were they happy to find that the main island could be seen?
6. How long did it take the boys to reach home?

CHAPTER 17

1. Where could the boys always find pigs?
2. How did Peterkin make shoes?
3. Why was Jack alarmed when he saw the canoes?
4. Where did the boys hide?
5. What weapons did the men from the canoes use?
6. When did the men from the first canoe run away?
7. How did the islanders from the canoes make a fire?
8. When did Jack shout and attack the islanders?
9. Why did the chief's men not help him in his fight with Jack?
10. Which side won the battle in the end, and how?

CHAPTER 18

1. How did Jack bring the baby's mother round?
2. What did the boys give the islanders to eat?
3. What did they do themselves while the islanders were eating?
4. How did the chief pronounce Jack's name?
5. Who was Avatea?
6. What was done with the dead bodies?
7. What did the boys give to Tararo?
8. How did they say farewell?

CHAPTER 19

1. Where were the boys when the ship was first seen?
2. How did the boys attract the attention of the ship's crew?
3. How did the boys spend the last day on their island?
4. What did they leave behind on the island?

SOME THINGS TO DO

1 Draw a large map of the island, and mark on it the various places and journeys mentioned in the story.
2 Make a list of the possessions the boys had when they arrived on the island, and describe the uses to which each was put.
3 Make models or drawing of the things which made up a "feast".
4 Collect some of Peterkin's jokes, and explain them if necessary.
5 Draw a sketch showing how the boys' boat was built.
6 Make a list of the most useful trees and plants the boys found on the island, and describe the use they made of each.